Elena Kincaid, Maia Dylan, and Sarah Marsh

EVERNIGHT PUBLISHING ®

www.evernightpublishing.com

Copyright© 2018

Elena Kincaid, Maia Dylan, and Sarah Marsh

Editor: Karyn White

Cover Artist: Jay Aheer

ISBN: 978-1-77339-623-1

Elena Kincaid, Maia Dylan, and Sarah Marsh

DEDICATION

Once again, we would like to dedicate this book to our Sinfully More Erotic Street Team members, who inspired this series. We love you guys and are so grateful for your friendship. And a special thank you to Julie and Debra for naming our two baddies in this book.

Elena Kincaid, Maia Dylan, and Sarah Marsh

BOUND TO THEIR FAETE

Beyond the Veil, 3

Elena Kincaid, Maia Dylan, and Sarah Marsh

Copyright © 2017

Chapter One

Corrine sat in the den with her niece, April, and with Erica. It had been two weeks since the battle that had taken place on Gabe's property, two weeks since Kheelan had been defeated, his insane plot for revenge thwarted, finally ending the reign of terror she had to endure at his and Alefric's hands for over a decade. And finding April after all this time had been a blessing. It almost made her feel as though she had her sister back once again. Corrine was still trying to help April recover what few memories that she had of her parents before they were taken from her by a madman.

Corrine looked over at Erica and April and found her heart swelling with happiness that the two of them had found their true mates. But underneath it all, for Corrine, there was always the empty ache for what she'd been denying herself ever since arriving on Gabe's doorstep and pleading for protection.

She could feel him walking closer toward her now. Even though their bond had been denied, she could always still feel him to a certain extent, as if the Goddess was trying to prove her point.

April and Erica went quiet when Gabe appeared in the doorway. He obstinately stood there unmoving, preventing not only Corrine from escaping a long overdue conversation with him once again, but trapping April and Erica in a very awkward situation.

Oh dear. It seems my Alpha has finally run out of patience. Corrine thought it was a marvel that he'd lasted as long as he had. It was just one more thing to love about him, that he'd given her as much space as he had simply because she asked it of him.

"I think it's time we finally had a talk, Corrine."

"There's that rotten word again," Corrine said matter-of-factly while turning to face the window instead of Gabe. "Time. There's not enough of it. I need more."

"What the hell does that even mean?" he snapped. "I have loved you for so many years." His voice cracked on a pained note.

Corrine glanced at the girls, and she could see how uncomfortable they were, having to be in the middle of this, but Gabe kept talking, his voice sounding strangled. It was *her* fault that he'd been pushed to this. Corrine knew she'd left him no choice really. She'd made an enormous mistake, thinking that she could manipulate the will of the Goddess, and now she didn't know how to fix it.

"I don't regret a single moment of loving you," he went on, "even knowing you are meant for someone else. I couldn't have helped it even if I *did* know when we first met, but you've had plenty of *time* to tell me, Corrine."

"It's complicat—"

"Complicated?" Gabe cut her off, raising his voice enough to make Corrine turn to finally look at him. The pain she heard in his voice was breaking her heart. "You owed me the truth, no matter how complicated it was."

"You're right," she said after a moment's pause.

Corrine was about to continue, but a commotion at the front door diverted all of their attention.

"Where is she?" a masculine voice yelled from the hallway. Corrine knew that voice, and it sent a shiver of awareness down her body.

Seconds later, *he* came barging into the den, pushing right past Gabe.

"Braxas? What are you doing here?" Gabe asked.

Corrine felt the blood leave her face as the other man she had been trying to avoid thinking about centered his gaze on her.

"We've been friends for a very long time, Gabe," Braxas said, still looking only at Corrine. "We've had each other's backs more times than I can count, which is why I left after the battle in the Fae realm." Braxas then finally turned to look at Gabe. "Out of respect for you both, I stepped away, despite how much it made my heart break to know my mate was in love with another man."

"*Your* mate?" Gabe's expression was a mixture of sadness and fury.

They both turned to look at Corrine as Braxas continued. "I saw her, and I knew. Then almost immediately after, we were fighting a battle. I felt the stab Kheelan delivered to her as if he had stabbed me himself, but then I also heard you cry out in pain, Gabe. She was then healed and the two of you were locked in an embrace, the love you had for each other evident. It would have been better if I had *actually* been stabbed in that moment and less painful for sure."

"Is this true, Corrine?" Gabe asked. "Is he your mate?"

Corrine couldn't find the words, horrified at what a coward she was being. She'd never meant to hurt him, but it seemed like that was exactly what she had ended up doing. Her lack of response must have said everything to Gabe. He shut his eyes and curled his hands into tight fists at his sides.

Goddess, why couldn't she find the words to explain this to him?

"You should leave … now," Gabe whispered through gritted teeth, his eyes still shut.

Corrine inhaled sharply. She wasn't quite sure if he'd been talking to her or Braxas, or even if he meant for them both to leave until he finally opened his eyes and looked directly at the other man, his wolf very close to the surface.

"Out of respect for our friendship, don't make me ask you again, Braxas."

Corrine stood up from the couch, horrified at the scene about to play out before her. "Stop it." Her words came out as a whisper. "Stop it," she repeated several times, each time her tone growing firmer, but her plea fell on deaf ears, especially since the two men were now growling loudly at one another, locked in a staring contest.

Braxas sounded more animal than human when he stated, "I am not leaving without her. Never again! She is my mate. We. Are. Bound."

Apparently, that had been more than Gabe could take, and suddenly both men were shifting, locking themselves in battle. As their growls and roars filled the room, the thundering sound of feet running on the hardwood floor in their direction could also be heard.

Suddenly the den was overflowing with people as Gabe's men tried to separate the very angry wolf and cougar. They looked as though they were trying to kill each other, which was yet another result of Corrine's hubris. When she'd first had the vision of her mate and the trials that he and his pack would be subjected to in the coming years, she thought she'd be strong enough to resist the pull to seal their bond. From the conflicting visions the Goddess had shown her, Corrine felt as if she had to deny mating with Gabe for the time being. She could not let that future play out. She had to protect him, and at the time, she also she needed his help in staying out of the hands of the Fae when Alefric had stolen the throne, especially since Gabe was the only one she knew she could trust.

So she had created a spell to subdue the mating effects, hoping to give herself and Gabe a little more time. As the months and then years went by, she had more visions which only became *more* complicated, not less. They had revealed Gabe lying bloody and broken *after* they had mated. Another war loomed somewhere over the horizon, a civil war amongst the shifters this time. Corrine found herself at the center of it. She saw Gabe's pack losing the battle, but in some instances, they were victorious. In both scenarios, however, Gabe did not survive. Then something in her present kept shifting the varying futures, like the two big battles that had recently been fought. Finding out that she had two mates instead of just one the first time she had laid eyes on Braxas, had been another shock to her. The visions altered again, only this time, she saw Gabe having a chance to survive.

"Stop them, Corrine," Erica prompted her from where the three women were huddled in the corner away from the chaos. "They'll only listen to you."

"Gabe, Braxas, stop!" Corrine yelled out, hoping she could get through the battle haze. "You are *both* my mates."

At her declaration, the room went still, all eyes shifting back and forth from her to the wolf and the cat, both of whom now stilled and stared intently at her.

"This is my fault. I thought I was doing the right thing, so I cast a spell to delay the mating drive, and now something has gone wrong," she confessed. Corrine figured she might as well do it in front of everyone since they'd all know soon enough anyway. The pack did not keep secrets well. "I had hoped the side effects were just affecting me, but I can see now that it was naïve to hope for. I'm so sorry."

Corrine couldn't even look at them after she apologized. She felt so ashamed. She had known when she found that book of dark magic in Kheelan's workspace in the dungeon before she'd made her escape, that it was not a power to be trifled with. Against her better judgment, she had taken it with her anyway. She knew before seeking refuge with Gabe that none of her spells or potions would mask the scent of a mate from a wolf, so she had gone to the book and found something that would.

Now that dark magic had taken hold inside of her, leaving her unable to remove it, and slowly but surely, it would end up killing her. That's what her sister Ilyra had meant by "her time was running out," when she'd appeared to Donovan and Jason in the Shadow Realm and asked them to deliver that message to her. The magic was also preventing them from moving forward with the mating, but the connection was still there, and it would drive all three of them to madness and destruction if she didn't find a way to fix it soon.

Corrine felt as if she did not deserve her mates at all. She had already betrayed them and put them in harm's way, and they hadn't even started yet.

Chapter Two

"I'm so sorry."

Sorry? She was sorry?

Corrine had just ripped his heart out of his chest and thrown it away and she stood before him saying she was sorry. Gabe was pissed. Hell, he was beyond pissed and sitting firmly in the category labeled homicidal. He wanted nothing more than to allow his wolf to rip the throat out of someone and bathe in their blood. And he had just the feline in mind.

But he couldn't.

Why? Because the woman he had given his heart to all those years ago was standing in front of him asking him not to. *Goddamn it!* Surely, when the one person you trust above all others turns out to have deceived and manipulated you in the most horrendous way, it meant you were allowed to flip them the middle finger and tell them to fuck right off, and that you could kill who you wanted to and they had no say in the matter. Apparently, Gabe was that much of a schmuck because he couldn't say no to *her*.

With a growl he embraced the flare of pain that accompanied his shift, pulling his wolf back within him. He looked around the room and caught the eyes of his men. With a flick of his head, he told them all he wanted them out. Donovan nodded then held his hand out to his mate.

"But I think I should stay and—"

Gabe let loose a growl, filled with his dominance. April immediately stopped talking. Her eyes widened, and her head tilted to the side in submission. Even the dominant little wolf had no choice but to submit now that she had officially become a member of the pack.

"Come on, my mate," Donovan said in a low

voice, and Gabe could hear his wolf in his tone. His Beta was not happy that Gabe had silenced his mate, but in that moment he didn't really give a fuck. "Gabe needs a moment to talk with his mate ... um, mates?" Gabe shot him a withering look, his growl turning feral, and Donovan immediately presented his own neck in submission. "Sorry, Alpha. Mate, singular for sure. No disrespect intended. April, come on, baby, let's give them a minute to talk in private."

Gabe waited as his men filed out of the room. He met the stare of the two other women as they walked passed him with one of his own. He had risked his life and his pack to help save both Erica and April, and he had a lot of respect for both of them for sure, but in this matter, they had absolutely no right to this conversation. He was aware that his *former* friend Braxas had shifted back and was standing just behind him. The two of them had been going at each other with the intent to seriously maim the other just minutes ago, and now, even with a truce, momentary or not, Gabe remained with his back to him. From the very feline-sounding growl that emanated from him, Gabe knew the move was recognized as the disrespectful act it was intended to be.

Within moments, the room was emptied, and Gabe stood staring at Corrine. Although there were two Alpha shifters in the room with her, Corrine's gaze remained locked on his. She obviously knew that he was the bigger threat in that instant. She always was the smartest person in the room, he thought.

"Don't you glare at me like that, Gabe Errikson," Corrine scolded as she crossed her arms across her chest and rocked back slightly on her right leg. With her arms the way they were and her hip jutting out, she was the picture of haughtiness that had his dick reacting the way it always did when she behaved like that. He grinned wickedly when her gaze dropped to his cock before quickly returning to meet his eyes. Color rose in her cheeks. "And you can put some damn clothes on, too. It is distracting and not something I want to see."

Gabe raised an eyebrow and shot her a look. "Really? Unless I am mistaken, and I never am, the room just filled with the most delicious scent of your arousal, and that tells me that you want to do more than just *look* at my dick."

Braxas stepped up to stand on his right, and Gabe tensed when Corrine's gaze flickered in Braxas's direction. Gabe waited for the slam of jealousy to rock him again. When Braxas had first announced his claim on Corrine, Gabe had been filled with a jealous rage he thought would drive him to eviscerate the man, but now, although it was still there, it was more of an echo of that first initial blast. For now, he steadfastly pushed away that thought and what it could mean.

Braxas inhaled deeply. "I'm afraid I am going to have to agree with Corrine. I don't want to look at your dick either, Gabe. It's irritating knowing you are getting aroused by *my* mate. And, Corrine, I can scent your arousal, sweetness, and it is indeed the most delicious aroma I have ever encountered."

Corrine groaned, raising her eyes to the ceiling. "Goddess, save me from overbearing *naked* shifters. I am not going to look or talk to either of you until you are both dressed, and we can have this conversation without your dicks waving hello at me."

Gabe had to bite back a chuckle as he moved to the sideboard that sat against the wall and removed two pairs of running shorts, flinging one pair at Braxas before pulling on the second pair. "There you go. All covered up. Now, explain why you felt the need to deceive me."

Corrine's gaze flew to his, and he watched as her face paled. "It was not a decision I made lightly. However, it was one that I thought I had no choice but to make at the time. I am so sorry that I deceived you, but I thought if I could fix it … if I could just make it right…"

"Why? Why did you *have* to?" Gabe asked, and paused waiting for an answer, but Corrine simply stared at him with a helpless expression. "Do you have any idea what that did to me? I have felt a connection to you from day one. You know that I've never tried to hide my feelings from you. I thought that there was either one of two things happening. Either I was so completely broken that the fates and the Gods deemed me unworthy of a mate—although the connection was so damn strong between us, I knew that I could have loved you forever even if you were not meant to be mine—or that there was a mate meant for me somewhere out there and I would have to face dishonor when I eventually found her and forced the breaking of *that* bond."

Corrine gasped. Her hand flew to her chest. "You would have done that for me?"

"I would have fucking done *anything* for you!" Gabe roared. "You had my trust, you had my confidence, and goddamn it, you had my heart. All of which you have just shat on because of your deception and your manipulation. Gods, do I even really know you?"

Braxas stepped forward. "Look, we are all overly emotional here. Perhaps we should take a moment to calm down."

Gabe growled as he spun in his direction. "You do not speak right now. I am this close," Gabe lifted his left hand, his forefinger and thumb only a millimeter apart, "to ripping your spine out through your throat. This is between me and Corrine. If you feel the need to speak in the next few minutes, ask yourself this: How would you feel in my shoes? If the woman you loved just admitted to magically closing the damn link that bound you to her as her mate so you felt *a fraction* of what you should in her presence, then announced that she was destined for two mates? How would you fucking feel?"

Braxas stared at Gabe and cast a quick glance at Corrine before returning his attention to him. Gabe watched as a myriad of emotions swept over the man's face before his expression fell into one of understanding. Braxas nodded and held up his hands in surrender. Gabe dipped his head in acknowledgment and turned back to Corrine.

Corrine had not moved, but her eyes had filled with tears, and Gabe had to fight the urge to go to her. "You know me, Gabe. You know me better than anyone in this realm, the Fae realm, or any that exist beyond them. There are always decisions that need to be made, and consequences that must be lived with. When a seer is faced with a vision of the future, and cannot see how it comes about, but they know that they must do everything within their power to change it, then they are forced to make decisions that will not only affect their life, but the lives of the people who mean the most to them. And you do, Gabe. You mean so much to me. I couldn't bear the thought of watching you die. As hard as it is to hear, if I had to make that choice all over again, I would have made the same one. It was made in an attempt to change the future and save your life, and I will not apologize for that. I am so sorry for hurting you, for not telling you sooner, but I am not sorry for trying to save you. You may not believe that of me right now, hell, you may *never* believe that of me, but it is the truth."

Gabe's heart began to bleed at the pain in her voice, but he could not bring himself to go to her.

Corrine turned to face Braxas, and Gabe saw the man visibly tense. In all of his loss and rage at what he felt as an injustice toward himself, Gabe had staunchly refused to acknowledge what Braxas must have felt when he turned his back on Corrine and walked away. Braxas was suffering, too.

Corrine took a deep shuddering breath. "I owe you an apology as well, Braxas. I felt the connection to you the moment we met, but I had no idea how to handle it. Erica was being held captive, we were about to go to war, threat after threat was coming at us, and I could not acknowledge our bond when I was hiding the one I shared with Gabe. I just couldn't do it."

Braxas's jaw tightened before he nodded and then seemed to relax. Obviously, for Braxas, just hearing Corrine acknowledge their bond was enough for him to move past the pain of her having to deny it. Gabe was envious of his ability to do that, but wasn't sure he could be that magnanimous.

Corrine turned back toward him, and Gabe steeled himself against the pain he saw radiating in her eyes. "I have not missed the fact that you have referred to your love for me in the past tense, Gabe. I am not sure if it is worse hearing it that way now, or knowing that you have never declared those feelings for me when you could have done so in the present tense. In the coming days, we will need to talk about what the future holds for this realm, the Fae realm, and the discovery that the Dark Fae still live. But for now, and before I can no longer do this in the present tense," Gabe knew what was coming and his entire being was torn in two—one half wanting to beg and plead for her to say the words, and the other half wanting them never to be spoken. "I love you, Gabe Errikson."

With those words still hanging in the air, Corrine stepped around him and walked out of the room, carrying herself with the grace and poise he had come to expect from her, leaving his heart to simply crack right down the center. His body filled with the visceral pain of heartache, and he did what all wolves did when they are hurt. He threw back his head and howled his grief to the world.

Chapter Three

Braxas wanted to rip out his own heart and roar up to the heavens along with the wolf, but he kept his cool. That was what his kind did after all. Cougars kept their emotions in check. They planned, they calculated, and sometimes, if it was strategically sensible, they even fucking stepped aside. He could only imagine the pain that Gabe was feeling, living with and loving Corrine all of these years under a veil of deceit, but hearing his mate tell Gabe she loved *him*, sliced Braxas open with jealousy and a pain he never even fathomed existed.

He knew that his own connection with Corrine had been instant and without a doubt, strong. It had also been completely reciprocated, yet he lacked the history with her that Gabe already had. Now he worried that she would forgo having two mates, and choose Gabe over him as Gabe would have forsaken anyone else for her. If she wanted Braxas, he'd stay and fight for her, to the death if need be, but if she truly did not, he'd respect her wishes and let her go.

"She won't, you know," he heard Gabe say behind him.

Braxas hadn't even realized he had walked to the window on the other side of the room, so lost in his own mental anguish. He turned around to face Gabe. "She won't what?"

"I know what you were thinking just now, Braxas," Gabe said, the pain still clearly evident in both his face and tone. "She will not choose me over you. I know Corrine. Despite everything, or maybe even because of it, I still know the way she thinks, and she'd sooner choose neither than have to pick between us."

I know Corrine. There was that same painful stab

again. Of course, Gabe knew her. She said it herself that he knew her better than anyone else. Despite the pain that Braxas felt, he also knew deep down that he could not separate them.

"I'm glad to see that you still want her then," Braxas admitted. "She seemed terrified that your love for her was in the past tense. I don't think she would ever recover from your rejection."

"Of course I still want her!" Gabe bellowed. "I hate what she did. I want to throw her over my knee and spank that pretty ass of hers until she loses the ability to sit down for a week. I want to tie her to my bed and make her squirm for hours, begging me to let her come."

Braxas swallowed hard picturing that scenario and found his dick straining painfully inside his borrowed shorts. He wanted to watch Gabe do it. He pictured Corrine's shapely red ass in the air and then his vision of her morphed into her lying spread eagled on the bed as Gabe brought her to the brink. He saw himself crawling in between her legs and devouring her sweet—

Gabe's laughter suddenly snapped him out of his reverie. It must have been clear as day to Gabe what his words had just done to him. And instead of jealousy this time, he felt a split second of camaraderie with Gabe. Braxas turned to face the window again and cleared his throat.

"Part of the reason I wanted to maim you," Gabe began hesitantly, "was because I saw the way that she looked at you when you walked into the room. She has been looking at me the same way for years." Braxas turned back around to face him as Gabe paused and dipped his head. "I asked you to put yourself in my shoes, and now I am putting myself in yours. You're the picture of coolness, and yet I know you're being torn up on the inside. It's like I can feel it now in my gut."

Braxas gave a slight nod. "I want her to be happy," he replied, his voice suddenly hoarse.

"You really are an unselfish bastard, aren't you? Kinda takes the fun out of ripping you to shreds."

Braxas snorted. "As if you could."

Gabe smiled, his face taking on a predatory cast. "Is that a challenge, cat?"

"Indeed." Braxas returned the same bloodthirsty grin. "As if I'd pass up the opportunity to go a round or two with another Alpha." No matter how worthy of opponents any of his pack members were, especially his tough as nails Beta, Katrina, they could all easily fall like dominoes under an Alpha's dominance. He was sure that Gabe could truly understand that. "But first, there is a matter of politics you and I need to address."

Gabe raised an eyebrow. "We have *other* matters to attend to now."

"That's precisely what I am referring to," Braxas continued. "I am assuming since you are alluding to the fact that Corrine will want us both as mates, and since *both* of us want her happiness above all else…" He let the sentence trail off as he gestured with his hand between them.

"If the fates have deemed us both worthy to be her mates then it must be so," Gabe acknowledged. "You were referring to what happens now with our packs?"

Braxas nodded. "You and I are both Alphas to very large and powerful packs. The logistics of running both packs and territories are something we can work out, but us joining forces in such a way will be perceived as a threat to some."

"This has to do with the conversation we had prior to you coming to our aid?"

"Yes."

Before Gabe had called Braxas for assistance with defeating the False King, Braxas had informed him of the rumors he had heard circulating near his neck of the woods. Rogue shifters, hungry for power, had been recruiting and growing in numbers exponentially. Without a True Alpha to lead them, they were reckless, and therefore extremely dangerous. Alone, Braxas and Gabe's packs were revered, but together they'd be frightening, most likely ending up with a giant target on their backs. Smaller packs may be persuaded through fear to join with the Rogues.

"Damn it," Gabe spat. Braxas knew he understood what he'd been getting at. "Corrine would be right fuck in the center of yet another battle."

"She said something about saving you, Gabe. She must have foreseen this battle, and the outcome for you must not have been a good one."

Gabe looked pensive for a moment before he spoke. "But she hadn't seen *you*," he said, and then he began to pace. "Corrine said she knew you were her mate when she first saw you at the house before the battle. The fates must not have revealed you to her before then, so that's why she only blocked me. And then she sought me out for protection. It all makes sense now."

"Great. Now fucking explain it to me."

He stopped pacing and went over to stand in front of Braxas. "I've come to understand a little about how her visions work. She usually lets them play out to determine the best path to take, especially since futures can shift so easily with a single course of action. She messed with it this time. The Goddess must have tried to warn her about this threat, and one or more scenarios showed me dead. She panicked and interfered, altering things so much so that it may have even prevented her from meeting *you* sooner."

"She must realize that now, only adding to her guilt." Something else she said suddenly occurred to Braxas. "Now we are armed with knowledge and we'll start investigating this new threat as soon as possible, but first we need to figure out how to make this work ... for all our sakes. She said something about there being side effects for the three of us. We need to—what is it?"

Braxas stopped talking. Gabe's face was suddenly devoid of all color, causing a panicked feeling to bloom inside his own chest.

"Fuck!" Gabe yelled. "I was so angry, so hurt, and so fucking busy focusing on myself that I forgot the other part of the message."

"What message?"

Gabe quickly explained about what happened to Donovan and Jason after Kheelan had poisoned them. How they were trapped in a Shadow Realm and that Corrine's sister, Ilyra, helped save them. She then passed along a message to her sister. The message was that her fate was bound to her mates and that *her* time was growing short."

Braxas felt his own golden skin go pale at that thought. He and Gabe tabled their conversation for now and bolted for Corrine's room together. He had only just found her, and an actual feeling of hope for his future with her began to blossom inside of him. There was no way he was about to lose her now.

He was toe to toe with Gabe as they threw open her door, bellowing Corrine's name.

"Where the hell is she?" Braxas roared when they found her room empty.

Several of Gabe's pack members rushed into the room, probably thinking they needed to break up another fight.

"Where is Corrine?" Gabe demanded, his Alpha at the surface.

"She said she was going for a walk," Roderick, one of Gabe's pack members, answered. And then he told them the direction she was heading: the clearing out by the old hunting lodge.

"I know where she went," Gabe stated. Braxas did, too. They did, after all, bring an entire army to that very location. "Go find April or Erica," he ordered Roderick. "We will need to cross the Veil."

When the pack cleared the room, Braxas grabbed Gabe's arm to stop him from leaving. "When we find her," Braxas began, "the three of us are going to have a long talk."

"Agreed."

"But first," Braxas let go of Gabe's arm and smiled slyly at the man, "I think we need to deliver that punishment you talked about earlier."

Gabe returned his smile, a wicked gleam in his eye. "Let's go get *our* woman."

Chapter Four

Corrine kept on glancing back over her shoulder as she ran through the woods. She did not think that it would take Gabe and Braxas long to figure out she had slipped out of the house. She needed to find a way to fix this, and the only person she could think of that would have any knowledge of the old magics or would know someone who might was Ishaya. Corrine had gone directly to the clearing and opened the portal to the Veil.

She squealed when she came face to face with a sword tip as she opened her eyes on the other side. She had forgotten that Erica's guards now protected this side of the gate.

"Oh Lady Corrine, my apologies," the young man in the royal uniform said as he held out his other hand towards her. "Here, let me help you."

"Thank you," she replied, taking his hand and stepping down from the stone steps.

"If you are here to see Queen Eyrica, I'm afraid she's still in the human realm."

"No, I am not looking for the Queen." Corrine stopped walking for a moment when she realized she had no idea how to find Ishaya, but perhaps this guard did, she thought. "I'm actually looking for Ishaya. Do you know how to find him?" She knew the forest folk kept their dens magically hidden, but some guards were now privy to a way to at least contact them.

The guard nodded. "If you walk down that path to the right until you reach the meadow, you can call out for him and he will come if he wishes to see you." He pointed to a well-worn path between two huge trees.

"Thank you." She smiled at him and was charmed at the blush that swept across the young Fae's face.

Corrine followed the path the guard had instructed her to, taking a deep breath of the forest air. She'd forgotten how entrancing and beautiful it was here, and it suddenly felt like forever since she'd basked in the heady magic of their realm. When they'd crossed over to join the battle with Alefric, the entire experience was a frightening and hectic rush. Corrine had never fought in such a battle.

She nearly gasped when she finally arrived at the meadow. It was awash in the bright colored twinkling of the starburst flowers. The bloom had been her mother's favorite, and it reminded her of spending hours with her sister as children, collecting the sweet smelling blossoms as a surprise to take home.

When she stepped into the field, a warm, soft breeze swept past her, and she could feel the spell within it. She whispered, "Ishaya," and waited as her inquiry was carried away through the wind.

Not five minutes later, the large man appeared at the edge of the field. Corrine walked to meet him.

"Lady Corrine," he said in surprise, "how nice to see you. Is there something I can help you with?"

"Hello, Ishaya," she answered. "I truly am in need of help, and you were the only person who I thought might have the knowledge to assist me. I need to undo a spell that has origins in dark magic."

"I see," he began hesitantly. He then offered her his arm to accompany him. "Let's go to my home and you can tell me more about this spell."

****

The outside of the forest folk's home was so disguised against the hillside that Corrine doubted she would have noticed it had she walked right past by herself, but the inside was reminiscent of the small cottage she'd grown up in. It had almost brought tears to her eyes when happy childhood memories rushed up to greet her.

"I just came back from the marketplace with fresh fruit cakes." Ishaya wordlessly placed the delicious treats on the table and politely ignored the rumbling of her stomach. She forgot the last time she had eaten. "Would you like some tea?"

"Oh yes, please." She sat in the enormous chair made to fit the man before her. In fact, everything in his home was scaled to his size, making Corrine feel rather like Alice in Wonderland after she had shrunk. "I haven't had Fae fruit cakes in such a long time. I managed to take some tea with me when I escaped, but the water is different in the human realm. The tea just never seemed to taste quite right."

Ishaya placed the kettle on the stove and then turned back to her with a sympathetic look. "You had to give up much when you fled our realm to escape Alefric." He spoke softly as he set the table. "I wish you would have sought our help. The forest folk would have aided you had we known."

"My visions were so confusing, and my window for escape was small. I just knew that I had to flee."

"Your Goddess did not offer you aid when you called to her?" he asked, sounding dumbfounded.

"Well, she doesn't exactly—wait, what do you mean *your* Goddess?"

The large man just looked at her and sighed rather loudly.

"It is shocking how little of your own history the Light Fae have retained over the centuries. I know that some of your kind were at least aware of the existence of the Dark Fae and as was intended, believed them to be long gone, but it seems that none of your kind even know the heritage, or that we forest folk are a part of it. For you and I do not owe our heritage to the same Goddess, although they are sisters. I believe we are bound to secrecy no more though, given these last events. Perhaps, we will once again be able to live as one people. Would you like to hear the tale of how the Fae realm was created?"

Corrine was speechless as she stared back at him. She wondered if her people could have actually forgotten their history. It was no wonder that some of the other races in the realm often remarked on the arrogance of the Fae, but she hadn't really thought about all of the reasons why until that very moment or that it extended to those who wished to live peacefully. Were they so sure of their own superiority that they had disregarded where they'd come from? The revelation that the Dark Fae were *not* indeed simply a myth told to frighten young ones to behave, but that there could be another Goddess in their realm was almost too much to believe.

Ishaya stood and walked over to an intricately carved bookcase, and he pulled what looked to be a very old book from its shelves. He sat it on his chair as he moved to pour the tea, and by the time he'd settled back into the opposite chair, Corrine was bursting with curiosity, hungrier for the knowledge than even the sweet cakes in front of her.

He opened up the book. "I could recite the story from memory, as my mother used to tell me the tale as a young cub, but I shall read it to you as it is passed on in the temples of the Dark Fae Dorum, who serve her will." At her look of confusion, he explained, "The Dorum are the wisest and favored sons and daughters of the Goddess, and the High Dorum are akin to the Alphas of our people if you will.

"In the beginning, just as all the Earth-bound

dimensions have their own beings of power, the Fae realm was seeded with glorious life by two powerful Goddesses.

"Two sisters, mirror opposites of each other in all ways. Allyria was the embodiment of the sun and sky, light and laughter, while her sister Ryssana was bound to the Earth itself and all its creatures. She was the shadow and darkness. Together they completed the balance and allowed all life and magic to thrive in the realm.

"But time makes even the most powerful of beings weary, and one day, the sisters decided that they wanted children of their own, fashioned in their image to love and nurture. Ryssana had sowed her forests and waters with all types of wondrous beings that served as caretakers to the realm, but still, they longed for more, and so the race of Fae was born.

"Allyria's children were fair of skin and disposition just as she was. They loved life with an exuberance that brought joy to her heart, and her purpose was once again invigorated. She blessed her favored with gifts of power and watched as they learned to wield them.

"Ryssana's children were fashioned as all of the creatures of the forest were, in various shapes and colors, but all were filled with a greater purpose than their own happiness. They were wardens of nature and the protectors of the balance just as their Mother was. Their gifts were aligned with the Earth and all her elements.

"As generations came and went, each race developed and matured, and the two Goddesses watched the journey of their children just as one would set free a flower blossom in a stream and watch its path in curious fascination as the water carried it away.

"They had blessed their children with free will,

and the realm flourished as they lived in harmony.

"Until one day, when a Light Fae magician unknowingly created a portal through the Veil to another realm. He became enthralled with this new discovery, his curiosity urging him to explore further as he crossed through and changed the fate of the entire realm.

"The Light Fae became enamored of the beings in this other realm, similar to them, but different in so many ways. They found the complexity of human emotions beautiful and began to bring them back across the Veil to keep as companions. The humans were unused to such raw magic and beauty as the Fae possessed and were powerless to defend themselves, becoming Fae-struck at first glance. Allyria was indulgent of her children as always. However, Ryssana warned her children that the humans deserved protection just as any other creatures and that they did not belong in the Fae realm.

"As the Dark Fae followed their Mother's word and the Light Fae felt it their right to do as they pleased, a chasm soon was created between the two races."

Ishaya closed the book. "The Dark Fae withdrew to their own hidden cities, away from the corruption of their Light Fae cousins. The rest of us who followed the Lady Ryssana tried to keep the human realm safe and apart from us. There has been word, however, that the Goddess has called forth her children to correct the damage done to the balance by Frederych and Kheelan."

"I'm speechless." It felt like an enormous weight to take in that the entire structure of her spiritual beliefs was only half of what the truth was. "I want to ask, how could our Goddess not tell us this, but that seems rather insolent to imagine she must tell us anything, isn't it? Especially given the fact how our kind previously behaved despite being armed with knowledge."

The huge man only gently patted her hand in

agreement.

"This spell you speak of," Ishaya began, peering at her intently, "you cast it on yourself? I can feel dark magic within you where there should be only light. Where did you come across the spell?"

Corrine was embarrassed to admit how foolishly she'd tinkered with an unfamiliar magic, but history was full of fools who did reckless things in the name of love. "The spell book was in Kheelan's possession. I found it as I was escaping the King's dungeons."

"You should have known better than to cast from it, Milady. The Light Fae are not meant to wield such magic. You have yours, and we have ours. It's not a surprise that it's gotten away from you."

"Can you help me to remove it?"

"I'm afraid spells of that caliber are far past my skill levels, but I can take you to a village where there are two Dorum who may be able to aid you. If they agree to help, you can petition the Goddess Ryssana directly through them. They are her High Dorum, chosen amongst our people."

Corrine felt such a relief inside of her heart at the thought that she may yet be able to salvage the bond between herself and her mates. She would do anything to save them, even if it meant giving them up.

Chapter Five

Gabe was heading for a stroke. His blood pressure had to be nearing nuclear proportions, and his wolf was shredding him from the inside. "Open. The. Portal." The growl of his wolf was so thick in his voice, his words were almost incoherent.

The constant grumble of the cougar shifter beside him would have been enough to put the fear of the Gods into any normal woman, but then again, the woman standing before them was no ordinary woman.

"I will not," Erica said in a tone befitting any Queen in any realm. She stood before the place he knew the portal existed, arms crossed over her chest. "Ever since Braxas turned up you've been throwing your Alpha around like it's the biggest butt on the dance floor. You had your chance to convince Corrine that she could be the woman to mate with two dominant Alphas, but *no!*" Gabe's left eye began to twitch. "Rather than try to see things from her perspective, and understand why she made the choices she did, you decided to yell at her and talk about your feelings for her in the *past tense!*" Erica took a deep breath, and then Gabe saw the conflict on her face. "Look, I'm not saying that I agree with her for not telling you the truth, but her visions ... Goddess, they have been such a burden to her sometimes. All she ever wants out of them is to protect the people she loves, and I think now she just needs to try and make things right. Maybe you two can just back off a bit and let her."

Gabe felt a small twinge of guilt burst to life within him before he quashed it. "Goddamn it, I was hurt, all right? She had years to sort out her emotions and talk to me about whatever the fuck was going on. Braxas and I had barely an hour! Then, she drops a bomb about how her actions were to save my life, and before we get the chance to talk more about this as a triad, she runs. We don't know if she's hurt, in danger, or what the hell is going on because that beautifully stubborn woman has decided to go beyond the Veil and seek answers to questions she has yet to share with us in detail. And from the message her sister gave to Donovan and Jason, I think her life may be in danger. Imagine how you would feel if it were Leo or Ben."

Erica hesitated, and her gaze slipped to her mates. Gabe could see that he was getting through to her.

"You don't know me," Braxas said to Erica, his voice intent, "and I don't know you, but at the request of the Alpha who governs over your mates, I brought those who are loyal to me to join the fight for you and your people. I say this not to garner your sympathy, but in the hopes that it speaks to my character. I tried to walk away from Corrine and give her time, and if you cannot understand the sacrifice of that, simply ask your mates." Again Erica's gaze flicked to Leo and Ben's, and what she saw there had her grimacing. "Corrine is my mate. She is Gabe's mate. And this situation is not what either of us planned. The three of us require time to navigate our way through this. Now, in order to do that, we need to find Corrine, make sure she is okay, and help her do whatever the hell it is she is doing. So please, open the portal."

"Okay," Erica said, dropping her arms to her sides.

Gabe wanted to throw his hands in the air and yell *finally,* but he thought perhaps that wouldn't be the best idea. He felt like Braxas hadn't said anything he hadn't said to Erica, just a little more … diplomatically, but the meaning had been the same.

Erica turned toward the portal and began to

weave her hands in a pattern that still freaked Gabe out a little as it looked odd, especially when you added in the fact that the air beyond her hands began to churn and shimmer out of focus.

"Alpha!" Gabe turned with a growl at the interruption and had to fight the urge to gut his second as he came sprinting in their direction.

"What the hell is it now, Donovan?"

Donovan slid to a halt. "You asked me to meet you here before you crossed the Veil to let me know about a situation."

The air split with Gabe's growl and the decidedly feline hiss of displeasure from Braxas, and Donovan held up his hands in mock surrender. Gabe remembered that he *did* ask him to meet him here, but he was too eager to get to Corrine. He filled his second in quickly on the earlier conversation he had had with Braxas regarding the Rogues and splintering factions. They were on the cusp of civil war, and it would not be long before word spread about their mating.

"Those fuckers want a war? Then that is what they'll get," Donovan said, finishing with a fierce growl.

"Agreed," Braxas said. Turning to Gabe, he added, "But not today. Today is about getting to our mate, making sure she is safe, and having that conversation we discussed. Then, when we come back here to deal with those who think to stand against us, we do it together. All of us, as the fates have decreed."

He stared at his friend and suddenly saw a surprising fringe benefit to this whole sharing his female thing. Gabe was the type of Alpha who often put his foot so far down his throat, he could kick his own ass for days, but with Braxas beside him, and the way that cougar talked nice to people, he could see him getting Gabe out of trouble on more than one occasion.

Gabe turned to Donovan. "You'll need to inform the pack and keep them in check. I know some of them are not above doing something stupid. Oh, and try not to act like a teenager who comes in his jeans the first time he sees a pair of naked breasts."

Leo and Ben both smirked and had to smother their laughter. Donovan was mated to a powerful half Fae wolf shifter, and April apparently had the ability to broadcast emotions to her mates. That was something Donovan had discovered the hard way when April transmitted a rather intimate moment between her and her other mate, Jason. It was so intense, Donovan had orgasmed in the middle of a meeting with Gabe and the other senior members of the pack. Something he was never going to let the smug wolf forget, as was his right as the man's Alpha and friend.

The sudden death glare Donovan threw in Leo and Ben's direction had them both fake coughing to cover up their laughter. Even as emotionally stressed as he was and the fact he was mere heartbeats away from either a stroke or a damn aneurysm, Gabe still had it in him to knock a cocky wolf back a step or two.

Donovan's eyes narrowed on him. "I will do my best, Alpha, and fuck you very much for bringing that up."

"Get in contact with my second, Katrina," Braxas requested. "She knows that I am here and that I will be out of contact for a few days. If war is coming, then the cougars need to mobilize, and she will know what to do. Tell her I want every cougar she can gather to be here when we get back."

Wolves were pack animals, and wolf shifters lived that way as well. The majority of Gabe's pack lived either on his property or very close by. Cougars, on the other hand, were solitary animals and although they pledged fealty to Braxas, some of them lived quite a distance from him and each other.

"Oh, Alphas?" Erica called, and Gabe turned to see a swirling vortex behind her.
"The portal is open. I have advised the guard on the other side to leave your heads on your shoulders. He will point you in the right direction."

Gabe stepped toward the portal, biting back his comment. No Fae had ever gotten the drop on him, and he certainly wasn't about to let one do it now. Despite the niggle of acknowledgment that came at the end of that thought, he refused to factor Corrine in that statement. With a nod at his wolves, he stepped into the maelstrom of space that existed within the bridge between the two worlds. He sensed Braxas making the transition with him, but he could not make anything out in the darkness.

When Gabe finally stopped tumbling, he found himself standing in the Elven realm. The Guard that Erica had spoken of stood a few feet away, and although he hadn't struck as soon as they materialized in the Elven realm, he certainly hadn't kept his weapon sheathed. *Smart Fae*.

Gabe took a deep breath, desperately trying to still the nauseating churn of his stomach and the fuzziness in his head that came with the transition beyond the Veil.

"You okay there, Braxas?" Gabe asked in a voice that remained steady by sheer willpower alone.

"Of course," Braxas answered immediately, but Gabe noticed his hands were clenched at his sides just as Gabe's were. "I could do that all day. Haven't you wolves ever heard? Cats *always* land on their feet."

Gabe grinned as he regained his equilibrium completely and could ease some of the tension he'd forced into his muscles to keep from shaking. "Come to think of it, I have heard of that somewhere. Now, let's find our mate. My right hand is just itching to feel her ass beneath my palm, and by the Gods, it is about time, too."

Chapter Six

"And how are these Dark Fae different from the rest of the Fae?" Braxas asked Gabe. They had been walking in the forest for about twenty minutes or so after one of the guards pointed them in the direction Corrine had gone. The guard had been cryptic about how they would actually get to her once they arrived at their destination.

These Fae beings were foreign to Braxas, especially the ones who lived in a forest that could have come right out of a childhood fairytale, and Gabe had just informed him of yet another kind during their walk—the dark ones. Gabe had also filled him in on the final battle and subsequent takedown of Alefric's right-hand man, Kheelan.

"I'm not sure exactly how," Gabe answered. "I know they have powers beyond anything I have ever seen, powers that Fae like Corrine cannot wield. She told us after the battle that she thought their kind no longer existed."

"And they don't turn to ash in our realm?"

Gabe shook his head. Braxas faltered in his step when he thought about Corrine turning into nothing more than ash before his eyes in the human realm. As if sensing his thoughts, just like he did earlier in the den, Gabe added, "She will not turn to ash in the human world either once we bind her to us, my friend."

Braxas stopped walking and turned to face Gabe. "Bound or not, no one will dare harm her as long as I draw breath."

Gabe placed his hand on Braxas's shoulder and looked him in the eye. "Not as long as I draw breath either," he declared just as passionately, right before he turned his head to the side. "Did you feel that?"

"I did," Braxas answered. He felt something in the air shift, and it had both men taking a defensive fighting stance. A slight ruffle of the leaves had the back of his hair standing up and his claws coming out. When he looked over at Gabe, he saw the man's eyes begin to glow and his canines lengthen. The pair of them positioned themselves back to back and made a slow circle, ready to pounce on whoever dared to sneak up on them.

Though shifter kind had made peace with the Fae that did not mean there were still not those amongst them who were still supporters of the False King, not to mention the discovery of these Dark Fae. Braxas knew better than to make presumptions about an entire race, but everyone was a potential foe until they proved otherwise.

He immediately began to strategize in his mind, calculating his next move with regards to the number of attackers, recalling Fae weapons and ways to disarm them. He thought about half shift versus full shift, his brain crunching numbers and scenarios all in a matter of seconds. He also made sure to account for Gabe's strategies. Gabe was fierce and would no doubt decimate his fair share.

As Braxas continued to plot, waiting for their attackers to strike, he heard booming laughter coming from his right and turned to face that direction, Gabe following suit.

A large bear of a man stepped out as if from the shadows and spoke directly to him. "What did I tell you would happen next time you came into my realm?"

"You told me you'd make me some of your famous homemade brew and we'd drink from sundown to sunup." Braxas retracted his claws and walked towards the big man with the large moving tattoos on his neck. When he reached him, he clapped the man on the back, who in turn gave Braxas what could only be described as a bear hug.

"Good to see you again, Braxas."

"And you, Grahame."

Grahame had fought valiantly beside him against Alefric's guards, and they each owed the other a life debt, to which his friend had said, "I reckon that makes us squared away, then."

Gabe had joined them and shook hands with Grahame.

"I have a batch that is perfectly aged for us," he said in invitation to both Braxas and Gabe.

"I'm afraid the ale will have to wait, my friend, but we can use your help."

"Do you know where we could locate Ishaya?" Gabe asked.

"What is your business with Ishaya?" Braxas could sense no apprehensive tone in the man's voice, but, though he and Gabe were known friends of the Fae, he knew Grahame still needed to perform his role as a guardian of the forest folk.

"Our business is actually with Corrine," Braxas told him. "A guard at the realm gate informed us she was with him."

"And your business with Lady Corrine is?" Grahame asked, continuing with his due diligence.

This time it was Gabe who replied. "Our business is to locate her so that I can take her over my knee and make her fine ass red for running away from her two mates."

Braxas smiled at Grahame and gestured between himself and Gabe as he added, "We're her two mates."

Grahame threw his head back and let out another

loud booming laugh and slapped his own knee. "Well, now that's as good a reason as any I've ever heard." He turned on his heel and led them down a narrow pathway, chuckling to himself periodically along the way. About fifteen minutes later, they came to a dead end, and Braxas had to do a double-take. Where there had been nothing but a mossy stone wall, now sat a small cottage.

Grahame clapped Braxas on the back, making him nearly lose his footing. Gabe thought he was being sly by taking the large man's hand, but Grahame, with a twinkle in his eye, shook his hand and then clapped him on the back anyway. Braxas could barely hold in his chuckle as Gabe stumbled forward.

"Good luck with that one," Grahame said before inclining his head toward the door. "She's a feisty one. I'll be expecting all three of you for a visit soon." With a final wave, he turned and walked back down the pathway, disappearing from their view moments later.

Braxas was about to do the polite thing and knock, but Gabe threw open the door instead and immediately bellowed Corrine's name.

And there she was, her face momentarily frozen in shock, some sort of pastry looking thing held midway to her mouth. Ishaya sat across from her at the large kitchen table looking … amused.

Corrine dropped the half eaten dessert back on her plate. "Overbearing Alphas," she mumbled shaking her head. She turned away from them, staring at her plate instead, and Braxas thought she looked as if she were trying hard not to cry.

"Yes, by all means, come in then," Ishaya muttered with a smirk. He may have said something about manners, but Braxas's sole focus was centered on Corrine.

Gabe stepped closer to Corrine. When he reached her, he knelt down on one knee in front of her and took her hand in his. This time, instead of being a quiet observer of the two and feeling like an outsider, Braxas moved to stand beside Corrine.

Gabe spoke first. "I understand why you ran, Corrine. I said things to you out of anger. I can't deny that I am still angry, but it pales in comparison to everything else I feel for you … in the present tense."

Corrine smiled sadly at Gabe before looking up at Braxas. "I messed everything up," she whispered. "My visions … I panicked. I—we—"

Braxas put his hand on her shoulder and felt her shudder beneath his touch. Her eyes widened. He understood all too well what she was feeling from their first contact. Electricity shot all the way up his arm, and his cock hardened at the thought of the sensations he would feel from skin on skin contact. He had to clear his throat before he spoke. "Gabe had already figured that part out, sweetheart. Perhaps we would have met sooner, perhaps not, but the three of us are here together now."

"They don't look to be at each other's throats to me, Lady Corrine," Ishaya said. He stood and went to place his cup in the sink.

Corrine looked from Braxas to Gabe and then back again, before finally looking down to stare at her lap. "I am going to fix this. I promise."

"*We* are going to fix this," Gabe said, gently tugging on her hand, prompting her to look at him. "All three of us. And, Corrine, you will never run from us again. Do you understand me?"

When she didn't answer, Braxas chimed in. "Gabe asked you a question, sweetheart. I think you should answer him."

"There is something Ishaya and I need to take

care of first."

Braxas was about to protest the fact that she was trying to exclude them once again, the stubborn woman, and so was Gabe by the looks of him, when Ishaya cut in. "I could not have chosen better mates for you, Lady Corrine. The Goddess herself has chosen two of the bravest, fiercest, and most loyal Alphas. I will help, of course, in any way I can, but it is their duty to protect you, and I'll not be party to excluding them. They are your mates, and they deserve to know everything."

Gabe stood, but kept Corrine's hand firmly in his. Braxas remained touching her as well. "What do we deserve to know?"

"There is a darkness poisoning her from the inside. It prevents her from fully bonding with you, and all three of you will go mad from it if you can't fix this."

Corrine looked down, but Braxas tipped her chin up. "Your intentions were noble. Do not bow your head in shame." Braxas then braced himself for the rest of what Ishaya had to tell them.

"If she does not purge the darkness poisoning her soon, it will kill her."

He and Gabe had already suspected that whatever it was she had done was killing her, but hearing Ishaya say the words felt like someone had ripped through his chest and placed a constricting hold over his heart. He had to momentarily shut his eyes.

"I'll give you some privacy," he heard Ishaya say before finally opening his eyes again. "Make yourselves at home. I have some business to attend to." He mouthed the word "brew" to Braxas before exiting his cottage.

Braxas took a seat next to Corrine while Gabe went to sit opposite her in the chair that Ishaya had vacated.

"It appears that the two of you have kissed and made up then," she remarked.

"We have," Braxas said.

"Tell us the rest of it, Corrine." Gabe folded his hands on the table. "All of it."

Corrine nodded and took a deep breath before she began. She told them everything, starting with the first vision she had of Gabe lying dead on the ground in a pool of his own blood. She barely contained her tears as she described his glassy lifeless eyes. In this vision, she'd also heard two men laughing, taunting her heartbreak. Braxas reached over and took her hand. Gabe mirrored him with her other hand.

The three of them sat there connected as she described the final vision she had before hastily taking action to prevent it. She saw other dead bodies of faceless men scattered around Gabe's. Though she could not identify them, she felt each and every one of their losses, almost as if she had known them. "They must have been the members of the pack I hadn't yet met.

"My visions started to alter years later after I had already tampered with the dark magic. I saw Gabe rising from the ground, bloodied, but the fire of life and battle were still very much present. I felt someone else in my visions, but they'd end before I could see the rest." Braxas squeezed her hand. "My punishment, I suppose for tampering with magic that was not mine to possess." She then told them about the fascinating origins of the Dark and Light Fae as Ishaya had just enlightened her with.

"So we start with these two Dark Fae," Braxas said. He was relieved that they at least had a plan in motion. He would not be able to bear the knowledge of her looming death without a prospect to prevent it.

Gabe nodded. "Agreed." He let go of Corrine's

hand and pushed his chair further out from the table. "But before we go, there is something I have been meaning to do for quite a long time, Corrine."

"Oh?"

Braxas let go of her hand as well, and she looked from one to other with suspicion.

"I think you need to be reassured that you belong to Braxas and me. That we are both fully committed to you."

"I believe you," she threw in quickly. Braxas assumed that she did not need her seer abilities to know where this was heading.

Gabe however, continued as if she hadn't spoken. He held up his right hand in a fist, his knuckles facing forward and popped his forefinger up. "You ran from us." Next up came his middle finger. "You didn't tell us where you were going." His ring finger followed. "You lied." Then his pinky. "You're very haughty." And finally his thumb. "You are way too stubborn for your own good." He tilted his now open and raised palm to the right, poised to strike a particularly beautiful derriere.

"Anything else?" she responded in exactly the haughty manner that Gabe's fourth finger had coincided with.

Gabe smiled slyly. "That's reason enough for now." He lowered his hand and placed it on his knee. "Hike up your dress and come lie across my knees."

Corrine leaped to her feet. "So you can spank me like some wayward child? I think not."

"No, so I can spank you like a lover spanks his woman when she aggravates the hell out of him."

Corrine's mouth opened on a silent O, and a blush swept over her face and neck. Braxas inhaled her sweet scent of arousal and felt the pressure of his cock straining against the zipper of his jeans. Gods, he wanted to be inside of her. "That shade of rose looks lovely on your cheeks."

Corrine's head whipped in his direction. "You're just going to let him do this to me?"

Braxas chuckled. "Let him? Hell, I encourage him. I have no doubt that all three of us are going to enjoy it immensely." He smiled widely at her. "Especially if that lovely rose color blooms across your ass as well."

She opened her mouth as if she had something to say, but shut it just as quickly. She took one step towards Gabe and paused, looking from one to the other. Braxas knew she was excited by the prospect of being spanked by Gabe while he watched, but he also sensed her trepidation. In the end, fear won out, and their little doe, temporarily mesmerized by headlights, broke her own spell and bolted out the door.

Gabe stared at the empty doorway as he spoke. "Tell me something, Braxas. Do cougars like the chase as much as wolves do?"

Braxas smiled widely again, but more for himself since Gabe still stared straight ahead. "Indeed we do."

It took only a few seconds before the pair of them, in unison, chased after her.

Chapter Seven

Corrine had the biggest smile on her face as she bolted out the door and ran frantically towards Ishaya and Grahame, who were both sitting on a couple of wooden deck chairs with large drinks in their hands. Both men laughed and pointed her to a well-worn path to the left of the cabin, and she sprinted off down through the bushes. Obviously, she knew she didn't have long before her wolf and her cougar gave chase, but that was part of the thrill, wasn't it?

She gasped when the forest gave way to a beautiful pond. Rays of sunshine filtered through the canopy of trees. The soft breeze was laced with the sweet scent of wildflowers, and the clear water beckoned her to linger and explore the breathtaking waterfall at the far end. She didn't have long to look as a rustling noise drew her attention to the woods once again, and then Gabe and Braxas stepped out of the brush with predatory smiles.

"Well, look where our little mate has led us." Gabe began to unbutton his shirt as they both walked towards her. "Did you know this paradise was here when you led us on this merry chase?"

"No, Ishaya pointed me in this direction," Corrine answered distractedly as Braxas also began to disrobe.

"I guess we really do owe that big bastard a round of drinks then, don't we?" Braxas said right before he undid the button on his pants.

Corrine was mesmerized as both men stood gloriously nude before her in the warm summer sun. They were works of art, their shifter genes ensuring the most beautiful male forms she'd ever seen. She took in the chiseled muscles, covered in lovely tanned skin. Braxas was a more golden tone, his body mostly smooth of hair, whereas Gabe was still darker tanned than her own moonlit shade, but he had a sprinkling of dark blond hair covering his pectorals and stomach—which led her to gaze directly towards his straining erection. Her body began to heat up, arousal making her heart beat faster, and the low growls that came from her men only stoked the fires higher.

"Undress, baby." Gabe's voice was strained with lust. "Let us see what's ours."

Corrine's brain wouldn't work. How could she think to respond with her usual witty banter while their bronzed skin taunted her to reach out and run her hands all over their chiseled bodies? She looked back up at Gabe, trying to remember what he'd just said to her.

"Cat got your tongue, baby?" he chuckled.

"Not yet," Braxas answered for her, "but I'm about to."

When he stepped up and ran his hands through her hair, she had to stop herself from sighing. Goddess, it had been so long since she'd felt the intimate touch of a man. But the touch of her mates was something else altogether, and when he finally brought his lips gently to hers, she did let the sigh escape into his mouth.

It was a revelation the way Braxas kissed her. He explored her mouth as though he wanted to taste every single inch of her, as though he *needed* to. Corrine had no choice but to return his passion. She could have kissed him for hours and was so distracted that she jumped a bit when she felt Gabe snuggle up against her back.

"You have entirely too many clothes on, my love," Gabe said as he reached in between them and undid the buttons on her blouse, "and I think it's my turn to finally have a taste of my mate."

Braxas slowly pulled away from her lips, and as he turned her in his arms, Gabe peeled away her top and let it fall to the ground at their feet. When Corrine looked up into Gabe's blue eyes, her breath left her for a moment. There had been so many times in the years since they had met that he'd almost been this close. She had known instinctually that he'd wanted to kiss her, and she'd also known that if she had allowed herself to taste him just once, that there would have been no denying what was between them. She would not have had the strength to keep him at arm's length.

Her eyes closed as he leaned in closer. She could feel the heat of Braxas's bare skin against her back, his hands softly caressing her hips. Gabe's hands came up to tangle in her hair as she felt the heat of his breath against her lips, but he didn't give her what she needed. He teased her with barely-there brushes of his mouth against hers. His tongue would dart out for a quick taste before he would move away, never giving up his control.

"Gabe, please…" She finally broke, moaning as she wrapped her arms around his neck and tried to pull him closer. The soft warmth of his chest hair felt incredible against her nipples. Having his skin up against hers was intoxicating in its decadence.

"Now and forever, Corrine," he growled in a low whisper, "you are ours."

"Yes."

Corrine felt the release of the waist of her skirt as Braxas got rid of the barrier that separated them, and as the material fell away, so did the last of her reservations. She would finally know the touch of her mates today. For the first time since her life had fallen apart all those years ago, when Alefric had slain her King and Queen, Corrine would take something just for her.

Her surrender was apparently exactly what the Alpha had been waiting for, because as soon as the word had left her lips, Gabe's mouth descended upon hers with determination. He kissed her like he'd been waiting a thousand years to taste her lips. At least that's how long it had felt like to her.

"By the Goddess," she heard Braxas purr in her ear as he rubbed himself along her naked back, "I can smell your desire for us, sweetness, and I can't wait to eat you up."

The soft warmth of his tongue as he licked her shoulder sent shivers down her spine, and she imagined how that tongue might feel in other places.

"We don't have to wait." Gabe pulled away from her mouth, leaving her breathless. "I want to taste you right now, baby."

Both men drew her down to the soft grass beside the water, and immediately Braxas claimed her mouth once again as his hands moved along her skin to caress her breasts and nipples. Corrine moaned when she felt Gabe's strong hands move up along the outside of her legs and softly urged them apart to make room for him in between them. The sensation of having their hands all over her at the same time was overwhelming. She desperately grabbed at the soft golden hair of the man who was now licking and nibbling his way down her neck, and when he finally reached her chest and sucked one of her erect nipples deep into his mouth, she involuntarily thrust her hips up, the sensation zipping all the way down to her aching clit. Corrine was soaking wet, and they'd barely just begun. She was having the damnedest time getting her hands to function properly, though she wanted to explore her mates as well.

Her hips bucked again when Gabe's hands finally reached the apex of her thighs and his fingers brushed up against her wet folds. A low grumble resonated in the back of his throat. The Alpha in him must have had enough of her wild thrashing. "Braxas, please restrain our mate while I make her scream for us."

The smile that bloomed over her golden mate's face was stunning, and she was distracted just long enough for him to trap her wrists and move them above her head before both of their attention was drawn back to Gabe as he lowered himself to rest between her very wet thighs.

Chapter Eight

"Damn, baby, look at you," Gabe whispered, and he could hear the reverent tone in his own voice. "Spread out before me like the most delicious temptation." Unable to hold himself back a moment longer, he lunged forward, placing his mouth on the most perfect pussy in the world.

"Oh, Goddess!" Corrine keened, and Gabe felt her body buck as she tried to move against him.

"Now, now, mate of ours," there was a definite thread of amusement in Braxas's voice, "there will be none of that. You will lie still and take only what Gabe gives you." Gabe heard Corrine start to curse aloud for a brief moment before her voice became muffled, no doubt by Braxas's kiss.

To take his mind off his own spiraling arousal, and the intense orgasm building within him, Gabe concentrated on pleasuring his woman. He used his mouth, his tongue, and his teeth to learn exactly what Corrine liked most. He took mental notes on what moves had her quivering on his tongue and which techniques had her rolling her hips forward to meet his mouth. Then he employed a mixture of all of them to drive her to the brink, over and over, before edging back a little, keeping her hovering on the periphery of orgasm.

He felt her tense for a moment before a fine tremble began to take over her body and he knew she was close to coming. He pulled his mouth from her with a growl, licking her sweet honey from his lips.

Corrine wrenched her mouth from Braxas's and cursed. "Goddess hex you, Gabe Errikson! Finish me, damn you."

Gabe loved the desperation he heard in her tone and reveled in the knowledge that he helped to get her to that state. "Oh, you will come for me, beautiful, but when *I* decide to let you, and not a moment before."

He gripped her hips and looked up at Braxas. With a flick of his head he indicated his intention, and between them, they had Corrine rolled onto her stomach, then up on her hands and knees in seconds. "Now, I believe I told you that you were due a little punishment, and I will not be denied a moment longer."

Corrine turned to look at him over her shoulder with a growl that had Gabe's cock thickening even further. "You wouldn't dare."

There was arousal and curiosity warring in her gaze, and Gabe couldn't hold back his grin. "See, now that is something you should know about me by now. I would dare, I do dare, and I will enjoy every fucking moment of it."

Corrine's eyes darkened even further, and she bit down gently on her bottom lip. Gabe shuffled behind her to kneel between her spread knees. From his position, he had the perfect view of her glorious ass, and he could see the moisture gathering in her pussy.

Leaning forward, Gabe lay over Corrine's back. He pressed his mouth close to her ear, groaning at the feel of his erection sliding through her wet heat. "First, I am going to spank your ass, making sure to spread the heat right around every delectable inch. You were made for me and Braxas, and that means you are going to love the hell out of this. You will want to come, your body will demand its release, but you won't. You will wait until I am buried balls deep in your pussy, and when I give you permission, you will come around my cock. I want to feel every fucking ripple of your first orgasm, and by the time I am finished fucking you, you will come for me a second time."

Corrine's breathing had changed to a helpless pant, and she made wanton whimpers of need that had sparks of arousal sweeping through Gabe's blood. Calling upon every inch of willpower he possessed as an Alpha, he pushed up and gently ran his hands over the firm flesh of her ass.

"Damn, Braxas," Gabe murmured. "Have you ever seen a more perfect ass in all your life?"

Braxas moved to her side. "No, there is no one that can compare with our mate."

Gabe had to agree. He raised his right hand, and without telegraphing the move to Corrine, or warning her it was coming he dropped his arm.

Smack!

The delightful sound of his hand meeting flesh filled the air, followed by Corrine's cry of surprise. Gabe held his hand on her skin, and rubbed the heat into the fleshy globe, making sure her cry of surprise ended in a groan of pleasure.

"You will not run from us again, mate." Gabe issued the second smack to her ass, being careful not to land it in the same place, spreading the heat once again. He listened to the sounds his mate made, taking his cue from her. "You were mine from the moment we met." S*mack.* "You were made for me," *smack* "and you were made for Braxas," *smack* "and from now one we will meet every challenge," *smack* "every threat," *smack* "every goddamn enemy that dares to come at us," *smack* "together."

Corrine's moans filled the air, and the sweet scent of her arousal was a heady perfume around them. Gabe's continuous growl that came from low in his chest told him his wolf was close to the surface as he delivered the last two smacks to his mate's ass, and rubbed the warmth into her skin.

"Mmm, your ass turns the most delightful shade of red," Gabe murmured. "Look at her, Braxas. Is she not beautiful?"

"So fucking beautiful," Braxas moaned, his voice hoarse. "That shade of red is now my favorite color." Braxas reached out with a shaking hand and gripped her ass, massaging her flesh in his palm. "Fuck, Corrine, I can feel the heat in my palm. You enjoyed that, didn't you, love?"

Corrine nodded. "Yes, I did … oh, Goddess. So hot," Gabe reached a hand between her thighs, sliding his fingers into her body. "Ah, Gabe!" Corrine yelled, desperation in her tone.

"So wet," Gabe growled as he felt her clamp down on his fingers, frantically trying to obey his earlier command. "All of this is for us. I will share it with no one but Braxas. Every drop of cream you release, every orgasm, every fucking fantasy you have is ours."

Gabe moved closer on his knees then plunged into her, driving forward in one firm thrust, burying himself balls deep inside of her. Corrine cried out, and he felt her inner muscles clamp down hard on his cock, strangling him with her need to stave off the release.

"Fuck," Gabe growled. "So fucking hot, so fucking tight. Come, baby, come for me!"

Corrine threw her head back and keened her release to the woods around them just as he felt her pussy ripple strongly around him.

He gripped her hips and began to move, pounding into her, using his strength to draw her body back to meet his thrusts. He maintained a punishing speed, holding off his own orgasm as he fucked her through her peak, then stoked the fires inside of her again. Soon, she was sobbing with need, and pushing her body back to meet his thrusts and he knew she was caught in the maelstrom of another impending release, and his inner wolf howled with satisfaction.

"Mine," he growled as he reached a hand around her, "my woman." His balls tightened and he knew he was lost to her, just as he had always been, but before he allowed his body the release it so desperately craved, he pressed a finger to his lover's clit, and felt her go over one more time.

"Corrine!" He roared her name as he exploded within her. His hips slammed into her, once, twice, three times, his body succumbing to the pleasure. He shuddered against her, and his hips rolled forward. He felt Corrine's arms give out beneath her, and he quickly sat back, pulling her against his chest so she wouldn't end up sprawled on the forest floor.

With his arms wrapped around her as they were, he could feel her heart pounding in her chest, and he sighed when he realized the speed and rhythm matched his own.

"I love you, Corrine," Gabe whispered, pressing an open-mouthed kiss to her shoulder. "You are my mate, I know you are, and as soon as we deal with this magical shit that I am still struggling to understand, then our bond will be unbreakable. I pledge my love, loyalty, and strength to you and you alone. I accept Braxas as your mate as well. He and I will work together to ensure your safety and your happiness for all time. That is my promise to you."

Corrine sobbed and wrapped her own arms around his. "I love you, too. I make that same pledge to you and to Braxas, and I know that no matter what path lies ahead of us, we will make that journey together."

Gabe closed his eyes for a moment, reveling in her admission. They were finally together, and all was right in the world. Oh, sure, there was the whole poison, hidden mating bond, imminent civil war between rival shifter factions, Dark Fae magical shit, and potential madness leading to death thing, but hey, no start to a new relationship was ever perfect.

Chapter Nine

Braxas saw new tears pooling in Corrine's eyes as she agilely, on all fours, crawled over to him in the grass, but not before Gabe gave her one more lingering kiss. "I need you, too, Braxas. Please." She whispered the last word desperately.

When she reached him, she shocked the hell out of him by grabbing his hard, thick shaft and stroking him several times before dipping her head and taking him into her mouth. She hungrily swallowed him down and moaned in pleasure as if he was the tastiest dessert. He curled one hand into her hair while bracing himself with the other as she hollowed out her cheeks on the way up. On the way down, she took him as far as she could go and let her hand do the rest, massaging him at the root. He watched in erotic fascination as she pleasured him, her free hand roaming, exploring his stomach and thighs. He heard Gabe's heavy breathing, indicating he, too, was enjoying the show.

Soon it became too much. Braxas needed to be inside her. He felt his own desperation growing and gently eased her off of him. He stood and picked her up, cradling her in his arms, and walked the few feet it took to get to the gleaming, crystal blue lake beside them. The water was cool, but not cold and refreshing to his overheated skin. His cougar purred at the combination of the exhilarating feel of the water and their mate's silky flesh against his own. When he waded in up to just above his waist, he shifted Corrine to straddle his hips and wrapped his arms around her waist pressing her hard against his straining shaft. He kissed her briefly before touching his forehead to hers, gathering his control, wanting to savor the moment.

Corrine wrapped her arms around his neck, and

with just the tips of her fingers, she stroked his shoulder blades. "Can you ever forgive me?" she whispered.

"There's nothing to forgive, sweetheart," he replied sincerely. He'd need to work harder to assuage her guilt since she obviously had not let go of it.

She sighed. "I'm not sure if I can forgive myself." She turned her head slightly to her left. Braxas followed her line of sight to where Gabe, reclining on his back, head propped up on a wad of their discarded clothing, was watching them. Braxas knew he was giving them some alone time and saw no jealousy, only quiet contentment on his face.

Corrine turned back to face Braxas. "I am not sure who I wronged more," she continued. "You … depriving you of time, forcing you to play catch-up, or him … giving him time, but torturing him with it." She laughed mirthlessly.

"And what about yourself, Corrine?" Braxas cupped her face. "I can't even imagine the heaviness of the burden of your gift. I know that I would have done anything to protect you if the roles were reversed, and no doubt that Gabe would have as well. Let go of your guilt and allow your mates to bear your burden with you."

"Just like that, huh?" She smiled up at him.

Braxas nodded. "Just like that. We have a lifetime now." He wiped away the tears that now sprang free from his mate's eyes and kissed her.

The slow, sensual kiss turned hungry quickly. Their lips and tongues collided in a fevered frenzy until finally Braxas could no longer prolong anything. He lifted her hips and impaled her on his aching cock. Her pussy, so tight and warm around him, made him feel as though he'd finally come home. She held on tightly to his shoulders as he pounded up into her and she strove from her position to match his movements.

They alternated between looking at one another and kissing passionately, tongues dueling, teeth clashing, getting accustomed to each other's taste. Braxas had intended to be gentle with her for their first time, but his best intentions quickly fell to the wayside as something visceral and wild took hold of him. Their joining was raw and primal, and his beast would have it no other way.

The sound of their heavy breathing was added to the soothing sounds of the nearby waterfall.

He felt himself on the brink of release, and could already tell that she was nearing hers. Their bodies were made to fit, he thought, already accustomed to the feel of her even though this was only their first time. He pulled her tighter and let out a growl, his beast echoing his sentiments, happy to be joined with his mate as well. "Ah," he breathed into her hair, "you feel so fucking good, Corrine."

He cupped her ass with one hand and pounded harder, and used his other hand to squeeze first one breast before sliding over to the other. Her nipples, hard points, tempted him. When he bent forward and sucked one of the peaks into his mouth, Corrine threw her head back and let out a loud moan. "Braxas … oh … Goddess … ah!"

He felt her spasm around him as his balls drew up painfully tight, yearning for release. He freed her nipple and claimed her mouth in a possessive kiss as he, too, found his nirvana. His hot seed filled her, and his cougar roared into her mouth. After a few more long and hard thrusts, they wound themselves tightly around each other until their quivers had finally subsided.

And then Braxas stiffened.

"What's the matter?" Corrine asked.

His gums tingled painfully, and he heard ringing

in his ears. His animal paced frantically inside him. The force of the urge to bite her, and the fact that something was preventing him from doing so, made him throw his head back and growl to the heavens. In his peripheral vision, he saw Gabe stand up right before he heard the splash of the water. Braxas, still joined with Corrine, was holding on to her for support when Gabe swam up beside them.

"Braxas," she said grabbing him by the shoulders and giving him a shake. "I don't know what's wrong with him." He heard the panic in her voice and wanted nothing more than to comfort her, but he couldn't speak just yet.

Finally, the ringing at least stopped. He gave Corrine a gently reassuring squeeze to her hip and then laid his forehead against hers. "It's passing," he was able to finally say, his voice hoarse and sounding strange to his own ears.

"You're bleeding, man," Gabe said.

Sure enough, he tasted his own coppery tang and realized that he had bitten the insides of his cheek and bottom lip.

"Let's get him back on the grass."

Corrine slowly extricated herself from him. They waded back to the water's edge where she and Gabe helped him out so that he could lie down. A few moments later, his teeth retracted back to normal and the bleeding had stopped. He swiped a hand over his mouth to wipe away the blood and felt his cuts slowly healing already. "I wanted to bite…" Braxas took a deep breath. The pain was still there, but it seemed to be receding. "Something prevented me."

Corrine gasped. "The poison. Goddess, I am so, so sorry. We should have waited."

"Don't, Corrine," Braxas said, waving a hand in dismissal. They couldn't have known that trying to mate would have triggered anything.

"Braxas and I pounced on you, remember," Gabe added with a chuckle. "My beast is very unhappy, too. He knows without a doubt now that you're his mate, but he can't sense you, which is probably why I didn't have the urge to bite you after we made love. He's pacing back and forth in agitation, though."

As if the point of their discomfort needed to be driven home further, Gabe suddenly doubled over in pain, clutching his stomach. Corrine's eyes widened in panic, but Gabe through gritted teeth tried to downplay his pain. Neither Braxas nor Corrine bought it.

Braxas shuddered thinking about the next stage, the madness that would come from the dark magic and its poison, and the one after that, the one that could ultimately take his newfound mate away from him—her death. After he and Gabe had recovered enough, though he still felt weak and imagined Gabe did as well, they cuddled Corrine in between them. With the soft grass beneath them, and the sun warming them from above, they fell asleep—a temporary reprieve before hunting down the cure and getting ready to face another threat, but Braxas gladly took what he could get for now.

Chapter Ten

Despite her concerns, Corrine felt a momentary contentment resting there in the cool grass, snuggled in between her mates. It was a stolen moment, one where they didn't have to worry about the journey ahead and what they might find at the end of it. Gabe and Braxas didn't have to worry about their packs. They could put their Alpha positions aside and just be men. As the sun slowly moved across the blue sky overhead, however, Corrine could feel the darkness inside of her growing— along with her guilt. Now that she'd finally joined with her mates, Gabe and Braxas both had already begun to show symptoms of the poison that had infected her. They no longer had the luxury of time. They needed to get this journey started.

"We need to find Ishaya and be on our way." She reluctantly rose from their arms and began to get dressed. "He said it would take us two days' journey to find the Dark Fae High Dorum."

"Two days' walk?" Braxas joined her in retrieving his clothes. "A car would be helpful in this type of situation now, wouldn't it?"

"You read my mind," Gabe chimed in.

"The Fae don't believe in polluting our realm like you have yours." Corrine tried not to sound accusatory, but this was one aspect of the human realm that she would never wrap her mind around. How they could have such a blatant disregard for Mother Nature and the gifts their Gods had given to them, she would never understand. "There are those who use carts to move goods and such, but the beasts that help, do so under their own agreement. We do not enslave animals for our own benefits." She knew she was being suddenly bitchy, as

Erica and April would say, but she couldn't seem to help herself.

"Are you feeling all right, babe?" Gabe came to stand next to her, a concerned look on his face. "You don't seem quite like yourself."

How could she tell them that it felt like a stake made of ice had taken up residence in her chest? Corrine hated being so weak, and she didn't want them to see her like this. She needed to have better control than this.

"I'm sorry," she said, taking each of their hands in hers as they left the sparkling water behind and made their way back down the path. "I swear I'm not trying to pick a fight. I'm just anxious to get to where we're going is all."

"We are, too, love." Braxas leaned over and gave her a soft kiss. "It'll all be all right, you'll see."

They were quiet as they walked back to Ishaya's cabin, and when they finally came upon it, the two burly men were still sitting in the sun, drinks in hand.

"There now," Grahame threw his hands up with a smile. "That looks like a trio who have kissed and made up! I bet you let them catch you, eh, lass?"

She couldn't help but smile back when he winked at her, but she did notice Ishaya's smile quickly turn to concern as he seemed to study her a bit more.

"We need to leave for the village," he said as he stood and dumped out what remained of his beverage, much to his drinking buddy's shock.

"Well, this must be important indeed if yer wasting good brew," Grahame remarked as he stood as well. He, on the other hand, chose to down the rest of his brew in one swallow. "Do you need any help, friends?"

"We're off to seek council with the Goddess Ryssana's High Dorum," Ishaya said, raising an eyebrow at Grahame. "I didn't think you were on good terms with

Aeron and Alak, but you are very welcome to join us."

"Och, those two are so uptight!" Grahame rolled his eyes and sighed. "But I suppose it's past time I settled our grievance anyway. How could I know that lass was their cousin? I mean, it's not like the Goddess speaks to us all, is it?"

Corrine couldn't help but laugh when both Gabe and Braxas tried unsuccessfully to cover their amusement at the antics of the two huge men. Truthfully, knowing there was some grievance as common as perhaps one of their kin's virtue, made the Dark Fey Dorum seem less intimidating to her, more human even. Up until this point, they'd seemed more like a myth to her than anything else, especially given that when Ishaya had spoken of them, mostly in hushed tones, in her mind they had become an entity unto themselves. It was unheard of for any of the Light Fae to converse with their own Goddess on a regular basis. Of course, that was also due to the Goddess Allyria's personality according to Fae history. The Dark Fae's Goddess Ryssana appeared to be the responsible sister out of the pair.

Nevertheless, searching out two beings of unknown power, of a race with which her only previous encounter had been in battle, was rather scary. She was suddenly very grateful to have the two large forest folk volunteering to take them to the village and introduce them.

"Thank you both for helping us with this matter," Gabe said to their two companions. He must have been reading her mind. "We are in your debt. If there should ever be anything we can do for either of you, you can call on any of my pack to aid you."

"And mine," Braxas added with a nod. "Shall we?" he asked, stretching his hand out to indicate that

Grahame and Ishaya should lead the way. "We're burning daylight."

As they walked along the narrow path, Corrine following the two large men, she looked back at her mates. She saw dark shadows under their eyes that hadn't been there earlier.

"Wait," Gabe said, halting their movements. "Do we need to take anything with us?"

The two large forest folk turned around and just smiled. Then Ishaya said, "The Goddess will provide." He and Grahame then resumed walking and led them down a new wider path through the trees.

The terrain was mild, but Corrine was growing very tired—too tired. She was a very active person who loved to hike and jog through the woods around their home. There was no way she should be this tired already. In the back of her mind, she knew the reason, but it was terrifying to admit that the poison was affecting her so rapidly.

The sun was just beginning to set over the mountains as they passed a small creek.

"I'm just going to grab a drink," Corrine said. "I'll catch up." She tried not to let them see how weary she was, but she certainly wasn't surprised when all four men stopped to wait for her.

Corrine knelt down and used her hand to gather the cool water up to her lips. It was refreshing and sweet on her parched throat. Perhaps she was just dehydrated? A tiny bit of relief unwound in her chest at that thought, that maybe she just needed rest and it wasn't a side effect of the poison.

She leaned in closer to the surface, intending to splash her face, when she noticed a small drop of something dark fall from her nose into the water below. Corrine brought her hand up to her nose and felt a thick wetness. She wiped it away and looked down at her hand. When she saw a dark, almost black-brown substance that was clearly more than just blood, the fear that they might not have enough time to fix her mistake nearly choked her.

Chapter Eleven

Gabe cast yet another look at his mate as their group walked through the Fae forest, concerned with how quiet she had become. He knew something had happened when she had stepped away for a drink earlier that afternoon, but she had blown off his questions and his concern. He knew that there was something definitely wrong. When she had walked back toward them, there had been a fear in her eyes that hadn't been there before.

He shot a glance to Braxas and caught his eye, and the worry he saw there mirrored his own. They were both concerned for their mate and had no idea how to help her. There was no way the two Fae folk who walked with them were oblivious to the tension building among them.

"Corrine," Braxas began in a quiet voice. "I can see that you are pained. Your fatigue is killing me. Let me carry you, love."

Corrine released a shuddering breath. "As much as I know that offer comes out of concern for me, my answer must be no. Do you think that I cannot see the shadows beneath your eyes?" She turned to look at Gabe, and his heart ached at the pain he saw shimmering in the depths of her brilliant blue eyes. "Or yours, Gabe? And what makes it worse is knowing that it was my actions that caused this to happen."

Gabe growled low in his chest. "We have talked of this, mate. We all know the reasons behind your deception. There is no judgment here. Let it go, and if you need help, then stop being a stubborn minx and let us help you."

Corrine's nose flared as she inhaled, and he saw that stubborn tilt of her chin that frustrated him as much as it turned him on. "I said I was fine, and I am. I can walk on my own, and as soon as I am feeling in the slightest bit fatigued, I will call on you, your high and mighty *Alphaness,* and you can carry my ass the rest of the way, but until then, leave me be!"

Gabe clenched his jaw so tight he swore he heard his teeth cracking beneath the strain.

"The poison is affecting her more than she is letting on," Braxas said as he stepped closer to Gabe. "We will have to stop for the night soon, and let her get some rest."

Despite the fact that Gabe just wanted to roar that there would be no stopping until they reached these Dark Fae, he nodded. Braxas was right. Corrine was tired, and her feet were beginning to drag. Gabe had learned from his father that sometimes it was the role of an Alpha to do what was right for the pack, and not just what the Alpha wanted. That sometimes it was best to defer to the needs of the many, despite it being the exact opposite of what he as a man may want.

The thought of his father had him frowning. Luke Errikson had ruled the pack with a fair and firm hand, and when he died the loss of such a great man had been felt throughout not just his pack, but many of the shifter factions throughout the world. When Gabe had stepped into the role of Alpha, he had been more prepared than most, but he feared he would always be compared to his father, and that scared the fuck out of him because he knew he would come up short.

He had many memories of his father imparting his wisdom, but one that stood out more than the others was the day Gabe had asked him what the key to being a good Alpha was. The man had stood quietly for a moment, the two of them enjoying the quiet of the forest that surrounded their home.

"Being a good Alpha is not just leading your pack to victory," his father had said when he finally spoke, "but ensuring that you keep the pack together until that victory is attained. The strength we have is in being a pack. Keeping everyone together, supporting each other, and laying down the law when needed and knowing when to do all of it, that is the key to keeping it all together. And that, my son, will come with experience."

"Gabe." Corrine's sweet voice brought him out of his memories, and he turned to look at his mate. "Would you like a drink?" She was holding out a water pouch that Ishaya had given her, and the apologetic look in her eyes told him exactly what she wasn't saying. It was very much an olive branch and one that Gabe would gratefully accept.

Taking the pouch, he leaned in, and pressed a soft kiss to her lips, frowning slightly at the heat he could feel in her flushed face. "Yes, I would. Thank you, my love." He took a quick drink then encouraged his mate to drink some, too. "Ishaya," Gabe called out and waited until the man turned to look at him questioningly. "Let's set up camp here for the night. I don't know about you Fae folk, but us shifters could do with a rest."

Ishaya's astute gaze slid to Corrine, and then he nodded. "I was just about to suggest that myself. There is a river nearby to replenish our water containers, and no doubt even Grahame will be able to find us some fish for dinner."

"Hey!" Grahame complained. "Why say it like that? *Even* Grahame. I willna only catch dinner, I'll cook it to perfection as well, and you, Ishaya my friend, will be forced to apologize profusely."

An hour later, with their stomachs full of the fish Grahame had promised, Gabe and Braxas convinced their mate to rest between them. Not that it took much coaxing. Corrine was beyond exhausted. He and Braxas had created a pallet from the foliage around them on the north side of the large fire the two Fae men had built, and although it was no feather mattress, their mate had drifted off quickly. Braxas had settled behind her and wrapped his arms tightly around her, following her to a slumber shortly thereafter.

Corrine whimpered in her sleep, and Gabe looked over at her. She was mumbling something, and he could see the slight sheen of perspiration on her forehead. She shivered and shook and mumbled again. Gabe had grown increasingly concerned as her scent had changed throughout the day. There was an acidic note to her usual deliciousness that had his wolf pacing in concern within him. Was it the poison? What other reason could there be for it?

Perhaps she is still lying to me.

The unwanted thought had his wolf growling low in his chest. That couldn't be. They had cleared the air between them, and there were no secrets left. His wolf could hear a lie, but could he sense an untruth to the point where the person's very scent changed?

Gabe growled in frustration as he leaned back against the log he had placed behind them. Everything was so fucking confusing in this place, and he looked forward to the day when he could get home to his pack. A civil war was coming to them, and he was here in the Godsforsaken Fae realm when he should be with his pack instead.

He scowled toward the two men on the opposite side of the fire. They were sitting close together, warming their hands in the direction of the flames, and laughing it up like they hadn't a care in the world. They also kept glancing over at him and whispering to each other.

"You will need to watch those two," said a voice sounding like it came from beside him. Gabe turned to look at the man who stood in the shadows, staring at Ishaya and Grahame, who still talked quietly together. "I do not trust them. They have an agenda that is not yet known. When they attack, and they *will* attack, you will need to make sure you remove the bigger threat first."

"Ishaya," Gabe whispered low, but the bear man in question still lifted his gaze toward him. Gabe held Ishaya's stare but kept his expression blank.

"Very good. I taught you well," the man said. His voice held a thread of pride in it that filled a dark place in Gabe's heart. "I am proud of you, son."

"Thank you, Father," Gabe whispered again and dropped his head to hide his smile.

Chapter Twelve

Braxas waited until he was sure that Gabe had fallen asleep before opening his eyes. He had heard Gabe having a one-sided conversation earlier, and with his long-deceased father no less. At first, before Gabe uttered the word "Father," Braxas had stupidly thought that he was on his cell phone. Impossible, since The Fae do not use such technology, nor have they cell towers anywhere. Gabe's madness had set in, and even now in sleep, Braxas could hear his paranoid mumblings.

"Laughing at us," he murmured. "Mean to kill us … stop Ishaya first." He said a few more unintelligible things, but then Corrine had moved closer to him and Gabe's ramblings ceased, replaced with a light snore.

Braxas sat up and looked over at Ishaya and Grahame, who sat by their own fire some distance away. They were definitely *not* laughing. They were looking at him with concern, probably wondering how far gone his own madness was. He felt it looming over him like he was about to walk off the edge of a cliff and fall right into it, although it was his beast he feared for most.

He had a theory about that, about why the poison may be affecting them all differently. He stood up, careful not to disturb Corrine and Gabe, and walked over to Ishaya and Graham, eager to get their take on his idea while he still had the capability to think for himself.

"How are you doing, my friend?" Grahame asked when Braxas sat down beside him.

"This darkness is affecting my cat more than me," he began. "I fear I will soon lose control and he will take over." What he didn't tell them, was the fact that he had a sense of what his cat *would* do. Right now, the furry beast wanted Braxas to drag Corrine away into the forest and fuck her senseless, to keep fucking her until whatever darkness lessened its hold on her long enough to allow him to finally bite and mark her. He knew his cougar would challenge anyone who tried to stop him, even Braxas himself. With shifters, man and beast were always connected. Braxas had never felt such a disconnect before, and it pained him, both body and mind.

When he had spoken to Gabe earlier, it seemed that Gabe's wolf was still somehow in control of himself, the reasonable one, and both Gabe and Corrine had started showing mental symptoms before Braxas had felt his own. He voiced this to the men and added, "I think it's because Gabe got the brunt of the dark magic spell since Corrine had him in mind when she cast it, and because she had used the term 'mate', it extended to me as well." He explained how he sensed her as his mate right away, but something repelled his cat from marking her and caused him excruciating physical pain. Gabe had also been affected physically, though in a different way.

Ishaya looked speculative. He then nodded and said, "It makes sense that it's affecting you differently, but it's affecting you nonetheless. Mates are the greatest gift from the Goddesses and Gods, and Corrine has tampered with it."

Maim them now while they do not suspect you.

Braxas startled. He barely recognized the voice of his cougar, the viciousness completely foreign to his animal. His inner self, though fierce in battle and in defense of those he protected, would never suggest harming a friend, especially in such a bloodthirsty way. His cat sensed his refusal.

I will rip you apart, too, if I have to.

Braxas gasped, and then he felt a heavy weight on his shoulder. Grahame had placed his hand upon it.

"Fight it, friend. It'll be over soon."

Braxas patted the large hand, still reeling from the betrayal from his beast. He had to warn them to be on their guard. "You both need to be prepared. Do whatever you must to stop Gabe and me and get Corrine to the Dark Fae." He saw the hesitation on his friend's face, a fierce warrior in his own right. "Grahame, you must protect yourselves and our mate at all costs. Promise me."

With reluctance, Grahame nodded.

You and I will have words, cat, when this is all over. Braxas knew he had no right to be angry and felt strange about it, like battling himself. He only hoped that when this was all over, he and his wayward fur-ball would be one once again.

The three of them sat silently around the fire, unable to sleep. The sun had just started to rise when he heard the commotion. Corrine was on her feet, her hands balled into fists at her side. "I said you will not touch me, you stubborn mule," she yelled at Gabe, who then also stood.

"Am I not your mate? Or have you lied to me again? You like to tell lies … don't you, Corrine?"

Braxas bolted in their direction just as the loud crack of Corrine's palm against Gabe's cheek reverberated around them. "Don't speak to me that way. It was our mating that accelerated these effects, and I'll not risk further repercussions to satisfy your libido."

Braxas, having reached them by now, was about to be the voice of reason, but instead of his calm reassurances that they were all not behaving like themselves, he let out a feral growl, followed by, "Kill them all and take Corrine."

It was his beast, only the words were no longer

just in his head.

Corrine gasped. "Perhaps I should let the two of you kill *each other*," she yelled.

Braxas, realizing that somehow he had transformed into a half shift, felt little control over his body, but his mind knew that Corrine had reached her breaking point. Even from the short time he had known her, he was certain she would never utter those words to her mates. His beast growled at her.

"Growl all you like," she said without emotion and folded her arms beneath her breasts. "I'll be dead shortly after. Why should I care?"

Braxas sensed movement to his left and right and knew that Ishaya and Grahame were preparing to take action, but then he looked over at Gabe, who now sported a wicked gleam in his eyes. His silent look had spoken volumes. He wanted them to band together one last time and kill their mutual threat, then … they'd take care of each other.

His cat was quite happy with this plan until a piercing scream sounded beside him. He turned toward Corrine to see her covering her ears. Thick brownish liquid poured from her nostrils. "Corrine," he yelled, shoving back his beast. He caught her before she fell, and a moment later, Gabe, too, was by her side.

"Corrine, baby, we're here," Gabe said. His voice was hoarse and unsteady, but he seemed back in control of his faculties at the moment.

Corrine blinked up at them both as Braxas tried to wipe away the liquid. It kept flowing, however, and then he saw the blood intermingled with it. His panic rose. "What can we do?" he asked her pleadingly.

She just shook her head and closed her eyes. Gabe gently shook her and whispered apologies, his tone as desperate sounding as Braxas felt.

"We need to hurry," he heard Ishaya say. "Pick her up and carry her."

Braxas looked at Gabe, silently telling him what he could not verbalize, that Gabe should carry her because he no longer trusted his cougar. Gabe scooped her up and tenderly kissed her forehead. He saw tears slide down the Alpha's cheek at the same time that he felt his own.

"Now we run," Ishaya said, "while the two of you still have control."

Chapter Thirteen

When Corrine had woken up to Gabe's wandering hands, she instantly flashed back to what had happened the last time they'd touched and she just panicked. She jumped up and swatted his hands away, her worry for his health now getting bowled over by sheer irritation that seemed to swell up from some place inside of her. But then his eyes had narrowed in suspicion and he'd accused her of lying to him.

The Goddess help her, she'd *lost* it and slapped her mate right across the face.

Inside her head, part of her was horrified at what she'd just done, but there was a new voice as well, one that egged her on gleefully to do it again.

These males don't know what's good for them. It's a good thing I'm in charge, the voice had said before she verbally set Gabe straight. The next thing she knew, Braxas was chiming in, saying ridiculous things, and she wanted to slap the both of them.

Then suddenly, it felt like someone had shoved an ice pick through her eye, straight into her brain. The pain was instantaneous and all consuming. Corrine had a split second to realize her legs were about to give way before the soothing darkness engulfed her, finally giving her some relief.

When she opened her eyes, she was no longer in the forest at all and her mates were nowhere to be found. Instead, she found herself in a rather cozy little cottage standing in front of a woman sitting by the hearth. Being a seer, Corrine had had many visions in her lifetime, so she knew the otherworldly feel of them well, but this one was slightly different from all the previous ones her Goddess Allyria had blessed her with. Normally they had a dreamlike quality about them. This one felt so real, and if she didn't know better, she would have thought she was truly standing there.

"Hello, niece."

Niece?

"Won't you rest by my fire and speak with me?" The stranger smiled and gestured for her to sit.

Well, I guess she's not really a stranger after all, is she? Corrine, very much intrigued, knew that she was in the presence of a Goddess, one that up until a few days ago, she had not known existed.

"Thank you, Goddess," she replied, taking a seat across from the beautiful woman.

"Please call me Lady Ryssana, Corrine."

Corrine smiled in acknowledgment, speechless at the moment. She studied the sister of her own Goddess, reflecting on how different they seemed to appear. Allyria, whose name she had heard for the first time from Ishaya's lips, who had never revealed her sister's existence or the existence of the Dark Fae to her Light Fae children, had never come across as so humble as the woman sitting before her. Corrine couldn't help the small feeling of disappointment that she had had to learn the history of the Dark Fae from Ishaya.

Lady Ryssana was dressed very casually in a tunic top and loose pants. She wore her long soft black hair in a braid that trailed over one shoulder. Her bronzed skin glowed in sun-kissed perfection, with a teasing of freckles across her cheeks.

Every time the Goddess Allyria had come to Corrine in her visions, she'd been luminous in her flowing gowns, long golden hair, and flawless moonlit porcelain skin, looking every bit the Goddess that she was. It was bizarre to see her sister, even with her otherworldly glow, looking like any other Fae woman, ready to attend to her day.

A wiggling blanket sitting in Lady Ryssana's lap snagged the Goddess's attention. She swaddled a tiny furry face, picked up a small bottle with a nipple attached to it, and brought it to the eager cub's mouth.

"This little babe lost his mother, so I am fostering him until he's strong enough to make his own way. Then I will let him go to live the life he was destined to," Ryssana explained as she looked lovingly at the little bear eating greedily. "My sister and I have very different ideas when it comes to how we raise our children. Allyria was never very interested in the daily struggles of her children. She chooses to let nature take its course, but if this cub ever called for me, I would come." She now looked back up at Corrine, her expression much more serious. "My Dorum have told me that one of my own has committed heinous crimes against human and Fae kind alike. Do you know of this, child?"

"I do." Corrine swallowed at the sudden raw intensity she saw in Ryssana's eyes. She could feel the power increasing in the air around them. "Frederych was working with Kheelan on something awful. They were abducting humans and using them to experiment on. He was mad in the pursuit of power."

"I see," Ryssana began, her expression getting darker, "and this Kheelan is one of your people?"

"He was. He's dead now." For the first time, Corrine felt shame in the actions of her people as a whole. The Fae in general since she'd been a child, had always thought themselves so above the humans, shifters, and the rest of the forest folk, but it was that exact hubris that led to the insanity and power hungry greed of men like Alefric and Kheelan.

A tired sigh from Lady Ryssana distracted Corrine from her own thoughts. "I have to admit, child, I never thought any of my own creations could ever disappoint me so. But I suppose that that, in itself, is the folly of every parent whose progeny end up with only the darkest of their own traits. I was so busy judging my sister's children that my own have suddenly run amok."

"We believe Kheelan and Frederych were working alone, my Lady, but they had loyal followers. If they were ignorant of the experiments, I do not know, but they are also now dead."

"Nevertheless, I see now that keeping my people separated from their cousins in an effort to keep their hearts pure was an error in judgment. Perhaps Frederych had his own agenda, yes, but I will no longer allow myself to assume that all of my children are infallible." Ryssana was suddenly looking at Corrine in speculation, and it made her quite nervous. "I see my sister's goodness in you, Corrine, and I am encouraged to hope that more of her children can be led to help rather than hinder. Their magic only began to abandon them when they lost touch with who they were born to be. You have a strong leader now, and she has the heart to lead all of the Fae into harmony. But my children still have strong magic, and I will send my most trusted warriors to aid you in bringing our people together once again."

"I am ever at your service, Lady Ryssana." Corrine bowed her head, while her heart pounded due to the favor she still needed to ask of her. "But, my lady, if I could ask for your help with something first?"

"Yes, my child?"

"In an effort to save one of my mates, I cast a spell written by the Dark Fae, and I am told my mates and I will not survive it if we cannot see it undone."

"You knew it was unwise to dabble in magic you are not familiar with, did you not?"

Ryssana certainly had the chiding parent tone down to a tee. Corrine was so embarrassed at what she had done, she could not even meet her eyes. She was shocked when the Lady's soft hands were gently at her chin, drawing her up to meet her gaze. Tears pooled in Corrine's eyes at the love and compassion she found in the Goddess's dark green eyes.

"I see that you have many regrets, dear one, and that you did what you thought you had to do in hopes of saving those you love." Ryssana wiped away Corrine's tears. "There was never such a foolish thing done in love, which love could not undo."

Corrine gasped when she absorbed the line of prose. "Thank you, Goddess," she whispered.

"Aeron and Alak will help you to undo the spell and heal the damage done by the poison. Once that is done, they will accompany you across the Veil to heal the rift between our people, as well as the shifters."

"So we will get to them in time?" Corrine asked desperately when she remembered how aggressively the poison was affecting her mates. "I fear for my mates. This poison has spread to them as well."

"My boys will find *you*, dear one," Lady Ryssana informed her with a grin. It appeared that she was very fond of her High Dorum. "They might be a challenge for you to handle, but do have patience with them. They are used to carrying the weight of their people on their shoulders, but I could not ask for finer warriors. They do not know it yet either, but their fate awaits them across the Veil."

Corrine raised her brows in surprise, but since the Goddess offered no further explanation, she did not pry. Their time together, it seemed, had come to an end. Lady Ryssana leaned forward and gently pressed a kiss to Corrine's forehead before the darkness rose up to claim her once again.

Chapter Fourteen

"...she's yours. Kill that cat bastard..."

"... you know that she is lying to you. Why bother trying to save her?"

"...trust no one, son. That is the one true lesson you have yet to learn..."

The voice was speaking over itself and all at once, clouding his mind in a haze of chaos so that forming a thought of his own was beginning to hurt. Gabe snarled low in his chest as he charged through the forest behind Grahame and Ishaya, fighting to remain in control. Whatever the fuck that poison was that had Corrine on the brink of losing consciousness, was doing one hell of a job on him as well. He knew his father was dead, but when he heard him so clearly in his mind, it was hard to remember.

He glanced down at the woman in his arms, and an ache pulsed hard in his chest. She was so damn beautiful, and it was a humbling thought that this incredible woman was his. When he had woken that morning, aroused and completely surrounded by her scent, the voices had been silenced and he was happy. He held the woman he loved in his arms, and all was right in the world. When she'd pushed him away the voices came back with a vengeance, and something had snapped in his mind.

Gabe groaned out loud at the memory. She had woken, her face flushed with what he'd first thought was arousal, but it should have been clear that the heat in her cheeks and her glassy eyes that glared in his direction were due to the fever that she was running. She felt hotter still in his arms now than she had this morning, and his fear for her grew.

"...but she is lying to you. She must be

punished..."

"Fuck off," Gabe growled low, desperately trying to ignore his father's voice.

Ishaya suddenly appeared at his side. "Hold fast, my friend, we are close."

"Let's hope so," Braxas said grimly from his place on Gabe's other side, closest to Corrine's face. "I am not sure how much longer I can control my cat."

"As long as it fucking takes," Gabe growled, "that is how much longer you can control your cat. We have no other choice."

"...kill that bastard cat. He wishes to take the woman for his own. Remove the threat, and you will not have to share the whore who has been lying to you..."

That. Was. It.

"Enough!" Gabe roared, his head thrown back, every muscle in his body tensed. "My father would never call my mate a whore. I am Gabe Errikson, and I am a fucking Alpha. I control who I am, what I think, and my actions are my own. Get the fuck out of my head! I am too damn strong and way too fucking mean to be controlled by nothing more than a Gods-be-damned voice in my head."

"Well, that is good to know." Gabe spun toward the voice that had come from the forest beside them. "The earth realm would have to have fallen a great distance if the shifters our Goddess considers kin could be controlled by nothing more than a figment of their own imagination."

Gabe's gaze narrowed on the two almost identical-looking men who had slipped stealthily out of the forest. Both men stood a few inches taller and had to have a good thirty to forty pounds of pure muscle on him. Although one had a goatee, and the other was clean shaven, they both had long, black hair, with a series of intricate braids that ran down either side of their heads.

They wore dark leather vests and pants, and from where Gabe stood, he could distinguish the fact that each of them had a fair number of weapons on them. But what stood out most for Gabe was the strange gray color of their skin and that each of them carried an impressive number of intricate tattoos

"Regardless," the clean-shaven one spoke this time, his hands casually tucked into the low hung belt her wore that sheathed a large black curved blade, "our Goddess said we were to help them."

"How mere shifters could be deemed worthy mates to one of our kind, of the Light or the Dark, I cannot say."

Gabe heard the flippant remark from one of the Dark Fae in his head clear as day, but he'd been looking right at them and he hadn't seen their lips move. *Tricky Fae,* he thought. He growled as he stepped forward, shifted Corrine over to his left side in order to free his right hand, and revealed his wicked as hell claws. "Why don't you come see just how worthy a shifter can be, dark one?"

Braxas placed a hand against Gabe's chest and gave him a concerned look. "Gabe, what are you talking about?"

The one with the goatee tilted his head and stared at him quizzically. "It's the poison. There will be no fighting it shortly."

"Do you think they wish to meet us in battle, brother? I'm unsure if they realize exactly who or what we are, let alone the fury we can unleash on weaker beings."

Once again, he seemed to be the only one to hear their comments. If Gabe hadn't been cradling Corrine close to his chest, he would have likely stepped forward and punched the goateed fucker. "Weaker beings? Who the fuck—"

Ishaya stepped forward, placing a hand on Gabe's arm. "The Darkness is toying with you, my friend, you must not listen to the voices," he said.

Gabe closed his eyes and swallowed hard. He wasn't sure what was real anymore. Ishaya released the grip on his arm when Gabe finally looked up at him.

"It is good to see you again, Aeron." Ishaya turned to dip his head in acknowledgment of the clean-shaven Fae. "And you, Alak. As I am sure our Goddess has told you, we have come to seek your assistance. Lady Corrine has taken ill, and we—"

"We know what the Fae seer has done, Ishaya," the clean-shaven one, Aeron, said.

"We are of the opinion that she should be made to suffer the consequences of her actions."

Gabe closed his eyes for a brief moment, trying to rationalize that once again this voice was only in his head and was not actually said by Alak.

"We are here to help her as our Goddess has bid us," Alak *actually* did say.

Gabe heard contempt in the man's tone, though it did not match the compassionate expression on his face, and despite his rationalization this time, his rage went from simmering to nuclear in less than a heartbeat. "If you let my woman die, I will rip your heart out through your throat before this fucking poison takes me with her."

Alak rolled his eyes and let out a breath in exasperation before he stepped forward to look at Corrine, who was still held tightly in Gabe's arms. He thought he saw Alak's lips moving, but he heard no sound and then his eyes darkened and turned fluid before they changed back to normal and lifted to meet Gabe's. "I *said* our Goddess has deemed her worthy of saving, and she has tasked us with doing exactly that and we have never failed her." His expression became concerned as his gaze lowered back Corrine. "We will not let your woman die."

"Although, there is a first time for everything." It was his father's voice he heard this time, and Gabe's heart stopped, his rage withering beneath the strength of his fear. He looked at Corrine and cried out. Her face had gone completely slack, and he could see she was barely breathing.

"Corrine!" He cried out again as he dropped to the ground, placing her flat. Braxas fell beside him, both of them reaching for her wrists, and pressing their hands to her face. "Please, please, Goddess, no. Corrine! Don't you dare leave me. Do you hear me?"

Gabe went to move into position to start CPR but then found himself flung backward by an unseen force that threw him against the trunk of a large tree and held him there.

"If you wish us to save this woman," Aeron began as he stepped up to Corrine's still figure then dropped to his knees beside her, "then you must let us do so. I have a feeling that neither you nor that feline shifter has the necessary control at this time to stand back so Alak will hold you where you stand until this is done."

Gabe thrashed against the tree, growling and snarling with displeasure, the forest echoing his grief. The only sound that rivaled his was the similar sound coming from Braxas, who was being held against the tree beside him.

Gabe watched as Aeron's tattoos began to slowly move along his skin. He took a vial of liquid from a compartment on the belt that he wore and then tilted Corrine's head back and poured a dose of the viscous purple liquid into her mouth. Aeron then reached out with both hands, and placed them a couple of inches above Corrine's chest, much like Gabe had seen Erica and April do when they were healing someone. An arctic blue light, brighter than he had ever seen emitting from Erica or April, shone through this man's palms.

"El hün der mách alün
Im lasto telin dán han kálad."

Gabe had no idea what language the Dark Fae was speaking or what the words meant, but Aeron repeated them over and over, the blue light radiating from his palms grew in intensity. Gabe focused on Corrine and prayed that he would see her chest moving. His heart felt as though it began to bleed when she continued to remain still. He was losing her before he had even had her. The mating bond between them was locked behind the spell she had cast, and he would never know what it was like to scent her and know she was his above all others. He was lost without her, and so he would follow her.

Corrine's body arched off the ground suddenly, her chest slamming upward, and he gasped. She screamed in pain, convulsing beneath the light, and Gabe began to fight against the magic that held him restrained.

"Corrine!" He roared her name. "Aeron, stop! Stop fucking hurting her. I am going to rip your fucking heart out. I will shred the skin from your body!" Corrine screamed again, her hands reaching out, and although Gabe couldn't be sure, it looked as if she reached out toward him And Braxas. "Please, Goddess, please! Stop, do not hurt her anymore. Give it to me. Give me her pain!" Gabe felt tears sliding down his face.

He heard Braxas shouting but had no idea of his words. Gabe could feel the warmth of blood on his back where he lost skin as he thrashed against the hard bark of the tree, but he felt no pain from it. Or perhaps it was simply eclipsed by the anguish he was experiencing in seeing the woman he loved in such agony.

Corrine suddenly threw herself to the side, and the horrific sound of retching filled the forest. From where he stood, he saw a black thick liquid spill from her mouth. This must be the poison that had been killing her. A small kernel of hope bloomed within him. He watched, bearing witness to Corrine's battle for survival and her formidable strength as her body strained, ridding itself of the toxin that had invaded her system, over and over, until she sank back on the ground, lying flat on her back. Her chest heaved, and he heard her soft sobs.

"Let us go to her," Gabe begged, uncaring that his voice broke slightly. "Please, let us go to her."

Aeron's face was damp with perspiration, and he was fighting to drag air into his lungs. Whatever the man had done, it had taken a toll on him also. A quick glance to Alak and Gabe saw he was in a similar state. However these High Dorum worked their magic, the chore to cleanse Corrine of the dark poison had been a strenuous one, and it obviously affected them both.

"The Lady Corrine will live," Aeron said in a hoarse voice, aiming the light over the pool of gelatinous liquid beside her, and it evaporated into nothing. Aeron then aimed the light over Corrine's face, cleaning all signs of the poison away from her. "She will be weak for a while, but she will make a complete recovery." He pulled his palms back, the light extinguishing almost immediately and looked over at Gabe and Braxas. "Had it taken any longer for us to find you, she would have been lost. No matter how strong the bond among the three of you, the casting of magic is not something to dabble in without extensive study."

Aeron stood up and moved away from Corrine. He nodded at his brother, and in that instant Gabe felt the invisible bond holding him captive slip away. With a cry he launched himself forward, collapsing to the ground beside Corrine. He gently pulled her up so that she was cradled against his chest, Braxas pressing in close behind her.

Corrine sobbed their names as she reached out to both of them. Gabe felt her trembling between them. He took a deep breath, possibly the first one he had taken since the moment he placed her on the ground at his feet, and stilled. Her scent exploded within him. He had always been affected by the intoxicating mix of orange blossom and cinnamon that was uniquely Corrine, but never before had it been so intense. His wolf wanted to wallow in the scent, get it all over him, and in that moment, Gabe's wolf confirmed what his heart had been telling him from the moment they met.

Gabe sighed and hugged her tighter to him.

"Mate."

Chapter Fifteen

Braxas wiped away his tears, uncaring that he cried in front of an audience. His mate was alive. That was all that mattered. Gabe's reaction to her scent, now that the spell was lifted, had also tugged on his heartstrings and brought back the memory of the first time her enthralling scent and presence had revealed that she was his mate as well. She turned in Gabe's arms to face Braxas and he reached for her just as she reached for him, but then her face transformed into one of horror and he found himself being flung back by an unseen force.

"Don't hurt him," Corrine screamed at the same time he heard the deafening sounds of feral snarls. He looked wildly around, desperately trying to find the threat until it finally dawned on him that he *was* the threat.

He found himself in a half shift again, his beast clawing at his own skin. *I will rip you apart, too, if I have to*, his cat had threatened. He was making good on that threat now. He heard a wolf growl low in his ear, an encouraging sound, rather than a threatening one. Strong hands held him down as a small, gentle hand rubbed his leg. He heard chanting somewhere above him, felt his chest rise with a pulling sensation, a bright light, and then his body sank in tired relief.

"You are one, once again." a voice said from above.

And he felt it. He and his cougar were finally back in harmony. He couldn't be angry at the cowering form of his beast in his mind's eye. He looked as beat up as Braxas felt, not to mention angry at what had been done to him, what he almost did. He could have hurt his own mate, and that would never have sat right with him. "Not your fault," Braxas muttered to his cat.

"Braxas, are you all right?" came Corrine's panicked voice beside him.

He sat up. He felt weak and dizzy, but he needed to comfort his worried mate. "I am now, sweetheart." He kissed the top of her head.

He looked over at Gabe, who was still in his wolf form, and nodded his thanks. Gabe gave a low growl in acknowledgment. "That was quick thinking, Gabe. Goddess knows what would have happened if they had to deal with both of us at once."

"What do you mean by that?" Aeron asked.

"His wolf is the sane one," Braxas explained. "My cougar went completely mad." His cougar growled in his head in response, clearly unhappy with the reminder.

Alak's eyebrows rose, and then his face contorted into determination. "Stay still, wolf," he ordered. He then proceeded to heal Gabe. By the time the three of them were fully healed, the High Dorum looked completely spent.

"We are in your debt," Braxas said to them.

"You are not," Aeron said firmly. "We do as the Goddess bids without accumulating favors. Let us go now. We have much to discuss."

Braxas wasn't used to taking orders from anyone, and neither was Gabe, but given the fact that these two Dorum had saved their lives, and he was just too damn tired to argue, he followed without a fight.

The Dorum led them to a modest sized cottage that seemed to appear out of nowhere, much the same as Ishaya's had done. The beautiful antiquated structure was made of stone with bright foliage growing around it, foliage unidentifiable to Braxas. Then again, most things he discovered in this strange place seemed foreign to him, otherworldly.

"Be welcome," Aeron said, graciously gesturing them to all step inside. Grahame, however, lingered in the doorway.

"Don't lurk," Alak snapped at him. "It's rude."

"Wasna sure your welcome extended to me," Grahame said, looking abashed. The big guy actually blushed.

Alak raised an eyebrow. "Is that because you acted like a complete bowsermuff with our cousin?"

"I didna know Aneena was your kin."

"What's a bowsermuff?" Braxas whispered to Corrine.

She put her hand against her mouth trying to stifle a giggle. "A silly animal that chases its tail all day," she whispered back. "The males … um … are known to try to mate with almost anything."

Braxas had to smother his own laughter at Corrine's description.

"And if she wasn't our cousin, would it have been okay to take liberties with her?" Alak's gaze narrowed.

"Well, now." Grahame appeared to lose his temper at the insinuation that he had done the female a disservice. "Aneena and I are both consenting adults. It's none of your bloody business—"

"Our Aneena has let it go," Aeron said, cutting off his brother in an effort to defuse the awkward situation. "And so have we."

"Speaking of Aneena," Ishaya began, "I hear congratulations are in order."

"Thank you," Aeron replied. "We are very proud of her."

The tension finally broke. Grahame stepped into their cottage and took a seat with the rest of them at the large round dining table off of the kitchen. Braxas made a mental note to find out what affront he may have caused their cousin. The congratulations Ishaya had given them turned out to be because Aneena had just been appointed as a Dorum after she had performed an act of immense bravery, nearly dying in the process in order to save two infants. The parents of the brother and sister, unfortunately, did not survive.

"Aneena suffers greatly from not being able to have saved the parents as well and feels unworthy of the calling of the Goddess," Aeron explained, "but we hope in time she will embrace that the Goddess has her own wisdom in all things, even when we cannot understand it at first glance."

"And what of the children?" Corrine asked. "Do they have someone to take them in?" Braxas squeezed his mates hand in support of her concern. He felt for the two young babes as well.

"They are safe and in the care of one of our Elders, but their fate is shrouded in mystery," Aeron went on. "Our Goddess needs something to play out first, but would not say what."

Aeron and Alak set out some strange looking, colorful fruit, and a light brown liquid. To help replenish their lost energy, Aeron had said, and the man definitely knew what he was talking about. The flavor of the drink reminded Braxas very much of a fine tasting aged whiskey. The fruit was deliciously sweet and juicy, enhanced by the flavor of the drink. He felt his energy returning within minutes and noticed color blooming on Corrine's recently pallid face. The dark circles under her eyes had also disappeared.

"Tell me more about this spell you used, Lady Corrine," Alak asked after he, too, had ingested enough food and drink to look replenished.

Corrine explained how she had stumbled upon the tome of old spells as she was escaping the dungeons in the castle years ago. She had tried to decipher the pages, poring over them for hours upon hours. The language had been strange, but there were certain words that translated, and when she'd been given the vision of Gabe's death, she knew she needed to do whatever it took to stop that outcome from happening.

"Why did you choose this particular spell?" Aeron asked her. "It had an extremely dark origin and it took a toll on us to remove it from you."

"It was the only one that referenced 'subduing the beast'. I thought that it would block the mate bond with Gabe until we could sort out the danger he was in."

Braxas didn't miss the guarded look Aeron quickly gave his brother. They knew something more about this than they were sharing.

Ishaya and Grahame filled in the parts they were witness to, including the battle with Kheelan and Frederych's sadistic experiments. They also recounted some of the symptoms the three of them had been suffering from on the journey here, shedding some light on his, Gabe's, and Corrine's skewed memory of the actual events.

Braxas could see the fury returning to Alak's face. Aeron's lip curled in disgust, and he practically spat his next few words in his foreign tongue. Braxas didn't understand the language, but by the tone and expression, it seemed like a string of curse words.

"Frederych is lucky that he is dead," Alak said, raising a glass and nodding towards Ishaya.

Gabe had filled Braxas in on the mysterious and evil Dark Fae who had assisted Kheelan, including the fact that Frederych had tried to force a mating between himself and Ishaya's sister, Arethusa. He had murdered the woman, and Ishaya had finally been able to get justice for his sister in the battle with Kheelan's forces. Without the extra defenses provided by Frederych, Kheelan had met his own fate in the form of three avenging Fae women, one of them being Corrine.

"Frederych," Aeron said the name in disgust, "was of the same opinion as your vile Alefric and Kheelan, but he did not only see himself as above shifter kind, but above all of the forest folk, and the Light Fae as well." He jutted his chin out towards Corrine. "That spell you used could have been intended to enslave shifters."

Alak slammed his palm down on the table. "He would have betrayed Kheelan in the end, but not before they succeeded."

"You said the spell was made to enslave shifter kind," Gabe said, "but it nearly killed us, would have killed us had you both not stepped in."

Aeron took a long swig from his glass before speaking. "It was only killing you because it was fighting the magic of your mating bond as well. When your kind mates, the magic inside of you that makes you able to shift is at its strongest. Heart, mind, body, and soul, all striving to one goal—to connect with your mate and complete you. Your madness was heightened because of your inability to fully join as mates."

"That spell," Alak continued, "was written with the intention to separate man from beast."

Multiple gasps went around the room as the information sunk in. Alak explained further about the rumors they had heard. A small group of rogue Dark Fae had been suspected of *experimenting* with vile spells, but they had also been very good at hiding and eventually disappeared altogether. "We never thought they could have succeeded in creating such an abomination, but it seems that they had. Without harmony between yourselves and your animal spirits, you would have been torn apart, weakened, subject to paranoia and the ability to be controlled through manipulation."

"Why did it affect us differently?" Gabe asked.

Alak shrugged. "That I can only speculate on. The spell had been cast out of love, not malice, by a Light Fae while written for the Dark, and targeted its subjects accordingly. The wolf could not sense his mate, so he remained in control without the compulsion to claim, while the cougar was forced to hold back from its baser instincts. Either way, the end result would have been the same and considered a success."

"Dear Goddess, and I used it on you both." Corrine shook her head, fresh tears pooling in her eyes.

Gabe and Braxas immediately set to comforting her, whispering reassuring words and applying gentle touches. There was no point in trying to convince her to let go of her guilt again, Braxas thought. She would need to learn to forgive herself one day. All he and Gabe could do was to reassure their mate that there was nothing to forgive.

It was also time to get back and face the threat that awaited them on the other side of the Veil, and to do that, to ensure that Corrine's original vision of Gabe's death did not come to fruition, they both needed to finally claim their mate and stand together united.

As if sensing this, Gabe said, "We need to be getting back to our people now."

"First you need to rest. You aren't fit to cross the Veil after what your minds and bodies have been through. Ishaya and Grahame will show you to the village guest cottage, and we will accompany you back across the Veil tomorrow as the Goddess Ryssana has requested of us." Alak's declaration left them no room for arguing.

"Yes," Aeron said. "I am afraid you have some hard times ahead of you, but your reputation as skilled fighters and shrewd leaders are known to us after your battle with the False King of the Light Fae." His eyes narrowed as he turned to Gabe, and as he spoke, the blackness of his pupils spread through the irises until they, too were engulfed in darkness, all but an arctic blue outline around the eyeballs. "Some warriors who fall may yet rise from the ashes."

A moment passed and Aeron's eyes returned back to normal. Corrine reached across Braxas to take Aeron's large hand in hers and squeezed. "Thank you," she said.

Aeron nodded. There was hope that not all would be lost in the coming conflict, but Braxas knew all too well about how one action could affect another. As leaders, he and Gabe would have to be methodical in preparation if they were to win. Perhaps they could even lessen the numbers on the other side if they could persuade them onto theirs.

The five of them stood to take their leave, but before they reached the door, Gabe turned to the Dorum. "How is it that Frederych is like you, but he could pass himself off as Light Fae?"

One side of Alak's mouth quirked before he suddenly transformed in front of their eyes. His shimmery gray skin turned into a light coppery tan and all of the strange looking tattoos had completely disappeared from his body. "It's called a glamor."

There was definitely a lot more to learn about these Dark Fae, Braxas thought. "You may not consider us in your debt," Braxas began, "but you have our sincerest gratitude regardless."

Chapter Sixteen

Corrine was still reeling at how easily Alak was able to change his appearance as they stepped out the door, and she certainly wasn't expecting to walk out into a bustling village full of forest folk since it hadn't been there when they first arrived.

"What the hell?" Gabe gasped as they took in the change. Braxas's eyes were just as wide as Gabe's were.

"The High Dorum are able to shield the village from outsiders when they wish to," Ishaya said, chuckling as he led them through the small cottages. "You are our honored guests now and will always be able to find the village when you come to seek us."

Small children were running through the main square, giggling and playing games. It appeared that dozens of various types of forest folk called this village home. Some were huge like their escorts, while others were small like the dwarves in human myths. There were even some who looked more animal or creature than humanoid, but all looked at them with welcoming smiles. Both Grahame and Ishaya greeted friends as they walked towards a cabin on the other side of the clearing.

"I didn't realize the forest folk lived in communities like this," Corrine whispered to their guides. "We always assumed you lived spread out in the woods."

"Some do. The forest has many hidden secrets. The Light Fae were led to believe what we wanted them to for our safety, of course," Grahame answered with a solemn look. "Would you have trusted Fae like Alefric or Kheelan with the location of groups of forest folk women and children if you were us?"

That was a question that didn't even need to be answered as far as Corrine was concerned, and she shuddered at the thought of what either monster might have done with that information.

"I'll ask one of the ladies to send some supper over to the cabin for you all as well as water for a hot bath," Ishaya said as he pointed them to the cheerful yellow door that was the entrance to a cozy little stone cottage. "I imagine you must be exhausted after the trials of the last few days."

Sweet Goddess, that was an understatement, Corrine thought. She felt as though the two days since they'd crossed over the Veil had been two weeks. She couldn't believe that the burden of that awful spell was finally gone for good.

"That would be wonderful," she replied and then leaned in and gave the large man a hug, but not before, for the first time ever, she saw Ishaya blush—which then made her mates and Grahame chuckle at him—which *then* had him muttering at them to "sod off" or something of the like. "How can we ever repay you both for being such loyal friends, Ishaya?" she asked as they embraced

He returned her hug, muttered that no repayment would ever be necessary, and then ushered her back into the arms of Gabe and Braxas towards their home for the night.

The charming yellow door of the cottage did not disappoint the expectation of what lay inside. It was a simple one room layout, cozy and well maintained, with just the essentials—a bed large enough to accommodate frames such as Ishaya's, a fireplace on the farthest wall with two benches in front of it, and a small table with four chairs filled the remaining space.

Braxas got to work making a fire right away, and before they'd even closed the door, two young forest folk women arrived and were all smiles, hauling a huge copper tub between them.

"Hello, guests," the more petite of the two, with skin the palest of blues greeted them. "My name is Laiyla, and this is Misha. We've brought you your bath."

"Hello," Corrine answered as Gabe and Braxas rushed to take the tub from the ladies, and set it in front of the fire. "Thank you so much for your hospitality. I'm Corrine, and these are my mates, Gabe and Braxas."

"If you will direct us to where we can get the water from, we will gather it," Braxas addressed the women, who were openly examining all of the clothes they were wearing with avid curiosity.

"Oh, there's no need to gather it." Laiyla smiled and approached the tub. "That is why they sent us!"

Corrine watched in amazement as the young woman closed her eyes and opened her arms, and as she brought them together, water began to fill the copper tub out of nowhere.

"That's some trick," Gabe said in an awed tone. "How are you doing that?"

"We are elemental forest folk," the other woman, Misha, said. Her skin was a deep charcoal gray. Corrine watched in fascination as she stuck her hand in the rising water and steam began to form, heating the water for them. "These are our gifts," she said as she finished up her task. "Laiyla calls the water, and I control the temperature."

"You're both quite skilled." Corrine was shocked at the ease with which these young women used their magic. Goddess, if Kheelan had had any idea while he still lived how much power these people had, he never would have rested until he'd taken it for himself.

"We've heard that the Light Fae have lost their magic. Is that true?" Misha quietly asked, as if she was afraid of calling the same fate upon herself.

"It's true that most of the Light Fae don't have any workable magic," Corrine answered, "but there are still a few of us who have retained ours. I am a seer, and our Queen and another of our pack are powerful healers."

"What is it like on the other side of the Veil?" Laiyla asked. She had now filled the tub and was examining Corrine's pleated jean skirt as though it were the most extraordinary silk. "Is it wondrous? I imagine it's filled with all kinds of machines and beautiful things!"

Both Gabe and Braxas laughed at her wistful expression. "There are many things that are different on the other side, but different isn't always better. Do your people not travel across?" Gabe asked.

"Oh no," Misha whispered, "It's forbidden to interfere with other portal folk unless there is an important reason. That's usually left to our Goddess's Dorum to take care of."

"Well, that does seem wise, considering all the damage that Kheelan and Frederych accomplished right under our noses," Braxas added.

Corrine hated to see the look of disappointment on their new friends' faces. "Well, perhaps things are changing and one day you will be able to let us repay your hospitality on our side of the Veil. Until then, when we next return, we will bring you some gifts. Have you ever had chocolate?"

"You would bring us this choc-olate, Lady Corrine?" After Corrine nodded, Laiyla jumped up and squealed in delight, hugging her tightly. Afterward, she pulled Misha towards the door. "We shall leave you to bathe now. My mother will bring by your supper shortly. Thank you for your friendship." The girls both added a wave before departing, shutting the door behind them in a whirlwind.

Corrine smiled wide, Gabe and Braxas mirroring her.

"Well, it's nice to see that teenage girls are the same on both sides of the Veil—all about the clothes and the chocolate," Gabe teased as he pulled his shirt off over his head. A wicked gleam in his eye told Corrine exactly what he had in mind for after their bath. "Time to get you clean, mate, and then Braxas and I can get you good and dirty."

"I love the sound of that plan," Braxas growled low as he came up behind her and wrapped his strong arms around her waist, nuzzling and kissing softly along her neck.

She sighed at how it felt to be surrounded by her men, as Gabe moved forward and his fingers found the closure on her skirt. He leaned into the other side of her neck and inhaled deeply, a low rumble echoing deep through his chest. "Mmm, I don't think I'll ever get enough of the way you smell, my mate. Now let's get these clothes off you."

Gabe's strong hands caressed her hips and ass as he let her skirt fall to the floor, pushing her panties to join it as well. At the same time, Braxas's hands slipped under her shirt, cupping her breasts, causing a moan to escape her lips as her head fell back against his shoulder. His cat must have liked the offering of her neck because his hands tightened, and he lightly bit at the juncture of her shoulder. It had her body responding with a warmth she was unused to. The sex before with them had been amazing, but this time, without the interference of the dark poison, Corrine knew this was how it was supposed to feel to mate for life. The entire universe was right there among the three of them, for in this space in time, nothing and no one else existed.

"I can't wait," she whispered desperately. "I need you both now."

"As we need you," Braxas said, grinding his hard erection against her ass, "but we only get to mate you once, and I would have it be so much more than a rushed occasion."

"So, we will love every inch of you," Gabe added as he tossed her skirt and underwear off to the side, "and then we will make you ours for eternity."

Braxas stepped back from her with a sigh, and he peeled her shirt off over her head, and then undid the clasp on her bra.

"You are perfection, Corrine. Have I told you that before?" Gabe gently pulled away the last piece of clothing from her and ran his fingers lightly along the side of her breasts.

She couldn't answer, couldn't form words at all in this moment. The tenderness and love that she saw in Gabe's eyes took her breath away. There had been too many times in the past years when she had despaired that she would never get to have this moment with him, and to know that *both* Gabe and Braxas belonged to her, as she belonged to them, almost seemed like a dream.

"The water's perfect, love." Braxas now sat naked on the edge of the tub, his fingers trailing in the steaming liquid. "In you go. We will bathe our mate."

Corrine smiled at him as she stepped towards the tub. She squealed in surprise as Gabe picked her up and delivered her to Braxas.

"Check the cabinet for towels and soap, Gabe," Braxas said as he took her from his friend and slowly lowered her into the bath.

"Oh Goddess, this feels amazing," she moaned as the hot water began to soothe away the last twenty-four hours.

Gabe came back with a small pitcher, a stack of towels, and two small bars of homemade soap. She could smell the sweet scent of wildflowers, and it reminded her of their first tryst by the waterfall.

Neither Gabe nor Braxas said much as they each took a cloth and a bar of soap and gently began to cover every inch of her. The looks on their faces started off as concentration, but as her body began to react to their touch, she could see the passion rising in each man's expression.

Gabe's strong hands finally made their way to her breasts, as if he'd been saving them for last, and she moaned as he leaned down for a kiss. He took his time, licking and nibbling at her lips. She tangled wet fingers into his hair to keep him where she needed him. Corrine was certain that Gabe knew exactly the moment when Braxas's talented fingers had finally stopped teasing her inner thighs and found her wet folds because her entire body lit up as he teased her with light circles around her aching clit.

"I think our mate wants to come," Braxas chuckled as her moans were heard even though Gabe still took her mouth.

"Do you want to come, Corrine?" Gabe asked after he pulled his lips a fraction away from hers. "Do you want to come on Braxas's fingers?"

"Please," she whimpered, as both men increased their attentions to her overwrought body. Braxas settled his thumb over her clit and slid two fingers into her waiting pussy, causing her eyes to close in bliss as he worked them in and out of her slowly. "More, Braxas, more."

"I'll give you everything you need, love," he answered before he added another finger to fill her up, and she felt other fingers circling the sensitive entrance to her ass.

She had been imagining what it would be like to have both men take her together, but she suspected with these men, the experience would be like no other.

"Yes," she moaned, opening herself up to him as he slid one soapy finger into her as his other hand continued to shuttle in and out of her pussy.

"Goddess, Gabe, she opened right up for me," Braxas groaned at the other man. "Our mate is so responsive. I can't wait to get into this tight ass of yours, love. It's going to feel so good for you, to have us both loving you at once."

"I'm so close." Corrine tightened her grip in Gabe's hair, causing him to growl once again, but she whimpered in disappointment as Braxas pulled back, leaving her aching on the cusp of orgasm.

"Okay, I think you're clean enough, baby." Gabe reached down and plucked her out of the still hot water and then set her down, her legs shaking.

Braxas wrapped her up in a soft cloth and patted her dry, not missing an inch of skin. She could tell from the mischievous grin on his face that he was enjoying her torment. "You know, cat, turnabout is fair play." She cupped his chin and kissed him. "I'd be careful about the teasing because I *will* remember to do the same to you."

"Oh I do hope so, sweetheart," he answered, his eyes gleaming mischievously, before taking her mouth in a thorough and deep kiss that left her breathless. "Gabe, why don't you lie on your back on the bed and we will give our woman the pleasure she's seeking."

Corrine's pulse began to race at the look on Braxas's face. It was clear Gabe didn't know what his partner had in mind, but he must have trusted him enough to know that they would all enjoy it immensely. Once Gabe had stretched his muscled frame out on the bed—his long, hard cock almost waving at her to join him—Braxas gave her a light smack on her ass.

"Up you go, love. I want you to straddle Gabe, but with your back to him."

That was an order she would gladly follow. She slowly sauntered up to the bed, licking her lips, imagining feasting on the man who lay there. When she reached him, she leaned down and took a long lick up the length of Gabe's cock, loving the way he moaned her name. Then snickering, she threw a leg over his torso and scooted down so that her soaking pussy was right next to his aching shaft.

She felt Gabe's hands molding her ass, and then she received another sharp slap to one of her cheeks. "You're such a tease, baby."

"You two started it!" She laughed at his muffled curse when she wrapped her hand around his cock and began to slowly stroke him, while rubbing him against her clit as well, seeing if she could finish what they'd started in the bath.

"Uh-uh, love," Braxas chided as he crawled up onto the bed in front of her. "Making you come is our job now. You wouldn't want to earn another spanking, would you?"

Just the thought of her previous "punishment" at their hands had her pussy aching in anticipation. She bit her lip thinking about how hard she had come.

"Seems like she's thinking it over to me," Gabe said, laughing.

"We'll remember that, but for now, how about we just make you come so hard that you see stars?"

"Yes, please," she answered breathlessly at the serious expression on Braxas's face. *What else would a girl say to that kind of question besides a huge, "yes, please!"*

"Gabe's going to fill up that sweet pussy for you, and then I'm going to suck on your clit until you come all over his cock." Braxas's gaze never left her eyes as her expression went slack, anticipating how good that was going to feel.

"You ready, baby?" Gabe asked her, and at her enthusiastic nod, he lifted her up just enough so that she could guide his swollen tip to her entrance. They both groaned low as she sank onto his thickness. "Sweet Goddess, Corrine, you feel so good around me. Tight. Hot. Like pure heaven."

"Now lean back against him, love." Braxas braced his arms on each side of her legs. "Just let us do all the work.

She completely relaxed into her mates' capable hands. She loved the feel of Gabe's hot skin against her back, and when he slowly began to move her up and down on his shaft, she couldn't believe how intense it felt to have him so tightly pressed to the front of her sheath, stroking exactly where she wanted him most.

"Oh Goddess, I don't think I will last long like this," she moaned.

"Let it come, Corrine. You'll come for us until I want you to stop." Braxas leaned over and sucked her swollen nub into his mouth, instantly causing her to scream out his name as she came in a furious rush.

Chapter Seventeen

Gabe tensed every muscle in his body as he rode out the intensity of Corrine's orgasm. He should have been a little taken aback with Braxas's plan. After all, the thought of having another man's mouth so close to his own cock had never done a thing for him, but knowing that Braxas's actions were for Corrine's pleasure and now feeling her pussy ripple so strongly around him, he was most definitely a fan. He was also looking forward to the chance to return the favor so Braxas could feel the way their mate's body applauded the move.

There was one thing he had not taken into account, however—the way her sweet pussy clenched so tightly around his flesh, and almost had him coming with her, but he had his own plans for the night and was bound and determined to make them come true. Gritting his teeth, he weathered the physical storm of her body coming around him.

"Wow," Corrine breathed in awe a few minutes later, and Gabe shared a quick grin with Braxas. "That was … well … without a word to describe it. Or at least my brain is scrambled to the point I simply can't think of a word to describe how incredible that felt."

Braxas leaned in and took their mate's mouth in a swift kiss. "I fucking love watching you shatter for us, beautiful. You give yourself to us so completely, that it wrecks me every damn time."

Gabe reached up and turned her face toward him with a cupped palm against her soft cheek, her flawless blue eyes softening with the emotions he knew were no doubt mirrored in his own. "You are my mate. I knew it from the moment I met you despite the fact that the bond between us was blocked." When Corrine's eyes dropped from his, he lifted her head gently until her gaze met his again. "You do not ever hide your eyes from us. We understand why you did what you did, and although I don't think you need it, I feel it is something you seek. I forgive you, Corrine."

"Me too, beautiful," Braxas added from beside them, and Gabe felt Corrine shudder above him.

Corrine's gaze lowered for a moment then lifted to lock with his. "But I hit you, Gabe. I am so sorry. How could I have—"

Gabe made a dismissive sound and shook his head. "Corrine, you hit a male who laid his hands on you without consent, then turned feral when you told him in no uncertain terms to fuck off. I would expect any female in my pack to do the same damn thing. Not to mention the fact you weren't exactly yourself in that moment. This is the line in the sand, love. Forgiveness given on all sides."

Gabe watched his mate carefully. He prayed she wouldn't give into the tears he saw shimmering in her eyes. He had no clue how to handle her if she gave into them, and a quick glance at Braxas told him his partner in this triad felt the same way. Corrine took a deep breath and closed her eyes briefly, and when she opened them, his heart stuttered at the heat that shimmered there.

"Claim me," Corrine said in a voice that seemed to roll over him like liquid sin and had his dick revitalizing within her. "I want to know what it is like to be claimed by the two men the Fates have blessed me with."

Gabe's smile was slow and wicked. Once again, Corrine had surprised him, and he had a feeling that was going to be a common occurrence in their relationship.

"That, I can assure you, Lady Corrine," Gabe murmured as he sat up and wrapped his arms around her, cupping her breasts in his hands, "will be our very distinct pleasure. Now, I have fantasized about this a time or two thousand, and we are going to need a little position change for what I have in mind."

With a groan, Gabe lifted her off his rock hard cock. He loved the way her pussy seemed to tremble and tighten as if fighting to keep him locked within. Once he was free, he turned to Braxas.

"Lie on the end of the bed with your feet on the floor, brother." Braxas's eyes shone with recognition of the endearment and anticipation of what was to come. Gabe stared at him for a beat, knowing the two of them would forever be bound together in the pursuit of ensuring Corrine's happiness and safety.

Braxas moved quickly to comply. "I think I know exactly what you have planned, and I whole-fucking-heartedly approve—" Braxas paused and leveled his gaze at Gabe, "—brother."

Gabe grinned in acknowledgment and then lifted Corrine with him as he stood from the bed. When Braxas was in place, Gabe moved to stand between his feet and carefully lowered their mate until she straddled Braxas's thighs.

"Hey," Corrine breathed softly and leaned over the cougar, giving Gabe an amazing view of her glistening pussy and the gentle sway of her back as she arched slightly.

"Hey yourself," Braxas replied, his voice a deep rumble, but Gabe heard the tension in it that signaled how turned on the man had become. It was strange, but the longer the two of them spent together with their mate, the more Gabe became aware of the connection that was building between him and Braxas. The connection was not physical or sexual, but it was there nonetheless.

"Corrine, I want you to lower yourself over

Braxas, take him inside that beautiful pussy of yours, and fuck him like you mean it." Gabe spoke in a voice that held a strong thread of command to it, and he reveled when Corrine immediately moved to comply with his demands.

"Fuck!" Braxas growled as Gabe watched their mate slowly impale herself on him. From his position, Gabe could see the small revolutions of her hips as she spiraled herself downwards until she had every inch of him.

"Goddess, that is the hottest fucking thing I have ever seen," Gabe murmured as he reached out and stroked his hand down Corrine's back, making her arch up against him like a cat.

"Trust me, brother," Braxas said in a choked tone, "it feels even better being a part of it."

Gabe laughed. "I have no doubt. Now, move on him, love, take him hard, and show him how much you love to fuck your mates."

Corrine's breathing increased, and she began to move up and down with sure movements, rotating her hips every time she reached the top, and Gabe could see her cream glistening on Braxas's cock. Gabe reached for his own cock, working his hand in strong, swift movements from tip to root, mirroring Corrine's movements as she began to move faster.

The two lovers before him both began to moan, calling out to each other, and Gabe knew that the two of them were fast approaching the point of no return. When Corrine started to slam her hips up and down in a quick frantic rhythm, Gabe reached out his free hand and pressed against her back.

"Stop," he growled and grinned when they both cursed in frustration.

"Gabe, please," Corrine pleaded so sweetly in a voice that trembled.

"Soon, my love," Gabe promised as he moved closer, sliding both his hands down her back to the firm globes of her ass. "If you are to take us both, then I need to know that you are ready for me." He let his fingers slide into the sweet crevice of her ass and lingered against the ring of muscle that surrounded her back entrance. He slid his fingers further forward, and coated them in his mate's cream, then brought them back to her ass.

Slowly but surely he worked his finger into her ass, being sure to take cues from her breathing and the trembling of her body, determined that Corrine would feel nothing but pleasure in this act. Oh, there would, of course, be a small bite of pain, but as far as Gabe was concerned, that simply added to and heightened the pleasure.

"Gods be damned," Braxas moaned, and Gabe saw the man's fingers tighten convulsively against the soft curves of their mate's hips. "Our mate loves having her ass played with, Gabe. She just flooded my cock with her hot cream."

Gabe grinned as he added a third finger, and began to scissor his fingers within his mate. "That's exactly what I was waiting for. Pull up a little, baby, let Braxas slip from you for a moment."

Corrine moved up but gave a low keening sound when Braxas slipped from her body. "Gabe, please. I feel so empty, yet so hot. I need you both so badly."

Gabe quickly slid his hand between her thighs gathering as much of her hot liquid as he could, and bringing it quickly to his cock, coating himself with her own desire. "I know, me, too. I fucking need you so damn badly."

With a hand that shook, Gabe pressed his cock against her ass, fighting the tight feeling in his chest. "Push out against me, love." Gabe felt her tense as he pushed against the tight ring of muscle, but he felt her obey his request. "That's it. Good girl. Take me in, love. Take me in."

Gabe pushed forward in steady thrusts, making sure to move forward in small increments. He was by no means an average size, and although he wanted his mate to feel that slight pinch of pain mixed with pleasure, he didn't want to really hurt her. Growling low in his chest, he fought to keep control of his lust, not wanting this pleasure to end anytime soon. With one more movement of his hips, he bottomed out, his thighs pressed against his mate.

"You have all of me now, love," he whispered, wondering if she would hear him over the pounding of his heart.

"Oh, Goddess," Corrine moaned gently, and Gabe stilled.

"Are you in pain? Should I pull out?"

"No!" Corrine frantically reached a hand behind her and gripped Gabe's thigh. "Don't go, please. There is more of a burn or a pinch than a pain, but I—I like it."

Gabe let out a breath he hadn't realized he had been holding. "Thank fuck for that."

"Gabe," Braxas said in a voice that held more than a slight touch of his cat, "if I don't get back inside our mate, I am going to bleed you. And if we don't get to the claiming part of the evening, I might actually have to kill you."

Corrine giggled breathlessly. "I must admit, I, too, am hanging on by a thread. I want both my mates. I want to be finally claimed by you, and just so that *you* know, I will be putting a claiming bite on you both myself before this night is through."

Gabe's wolf growled happily at that thought.

"Cougars don't just bite, love," Braxas informed them both. "I'm a cat, and cats scratch. You will wear my bite on your neck, Corrine, and it will be four claw marks over your clavicle that will tell every shifter that sees them that you belong to me."

Gabe moved with her when Corrine slid down to take Braxas into her once more. All three of them cried out at the feeling. With Braxas in her pussy, Corrine's ass tightened to almost painful proportions around his dick.

Corrine whimpered. "Full. So completely wonderfully full."

Gabe leaned forward so that his chest was pressed to her back, and his mouth was close to her ear. "Hold on, love."

Gabe began to move within her, both he and Braxas timing their thrusts together for a while, driving the arousal to greater heights, but after a few moments, it was impossible to maintain any type of rhythm, not when the pleasure was building to a pinnacle he had never known to exist before, and his orgasm was rushing toward him with the speed and strength of a category five tornado.

He began to slam into his mate and was vaguely aware that Braxas was doing them same from beneath her. The two of them were moving with force into her, and from the keening sounds their mate was making, she was close to succumbing to the maelstrom of pleasure.

Gabe was determined that Corrine would go over first. He wanted nothing more than to feel the first shudders of her release before he lost his mind to his own. Just when he thought he was going to lose the opportunity, Corrine tensed even further then threw her head back to scream her pleasure to the room. He felt her ass contract around him, and he roared at the feel of it, and his canines slipped down just as his orgasm crashed over him. He leaned forward and clamped his mouth against the tender flesh of her shoulder, driving his teeth into her flesh and drawing her blood into his mouth.

The sensation of the mating bond slamming into place had his mate shuddering powerfully beneath him, but he held her to him, thrusting again and again into her ass as his body released a second time. This was the moment he had wanted with this woman more than anything from the instant he had met her but had never thought possible. And now that it was here, it was more powerful and emotionally consuming than he had ever imagined.

He collapsed onto his arms and leaned further onto her where she had slumped against Braxas. He growled against her flesh as he laved the bite mark he had made with his tongue, noting that he had bitten her hard, marking her almost viciously. "Are you okay, baby?" He winced at how hoarse he sounded.

"Mmmm," was the only sound she made. Gabe would have asked what she meant by that, but he felt the wave of satisfaction and love that flooded the bond that now connected them, and his heart swelled.

"Mate," Gabe sighed as he pressed a few kisses to the satin skin across her shoulders.

"Mate," Braxas growled from beneath them, and Gabe leaned up to see the man licking along the other side of Corrine's neck. No doubt he had also marked her as he said he would, and would lap at the wounds to heal them.

Corrine sighed as she moved between them, and Gabe pushed up to give her room to move. He wasn't quite ready to pull from her completely, and if truth be told, he didn't know if his legs could hold him if he tried.

"Mates," Corrine almost purred with satisfaction and Gabe grinned.

"That's right, baby," Gabe answered smugly. "You've got yourself two mates, who will love, protect, and cherish you for the rest of your life."

"Not to mention give you anything you want as long as it makes you happy," Braxas added.

"Is that true?" Corrine asked and turned her head so she could look at both him and Braxas when they both nodded. "Then there is something that I want right now, that will make me very happy."

Gabe frowned. "What is that, baby?"

Corrine looked between him and Braxas and swept her tongue over her lower lip in a move that had arousal swirling within him once more. "I want to do that again, but this time, I want to claim each of you."

Gabe grinned. His mate was perfect for him and Braxas, and tonight there was no oncoming shifter war in their realm, there was no duel between Light and Dark, there was simply Corrine—a woman who held his heart just as surely as she held his future.

Chapter Eighteen

Corrine lay peacefully in between Braxas and Gabe, sporting their mating marks. The mark she had given him still tingled on his neck, and the memory of that moment when she had sunk her teeth into his flesh deliciously lingered. She was finally his.

She turned in his arms, surprising him that she was still awake. "Can't sleep?" she asked.

In truth, he was exhausted. After they had mated and then made love to her again, their dinner had been waiting for them outside the door, just like the young women had promised them. They enjoyed a leisurely meal in bed, after which, Braxas and Gabe had taken Corrine several more times throughout the night before surrendering to their bodies' need for sleep. His arms and legs had felt like jelly and his eyelids were growing heavy, but the joy of watching his mate in her peaceful state a little longer had kept him awake. She smiled sleepily at him when he told her so.

"Do you really forgive me, too?" she whispered.

"I truly do," he replied without hesitation. He had already told her so earlier after Gabe had said it, but it seemed she had more on her mind.

"I just want you to know how much you mean to me," she continued. "I've known you only a short while and we have so much to learn about one another, but you need to know that you are just as dear to me as Gabe is." She paused and took a deep breath before adding, "I love you, Braxas."

Braxas touched his forehead to hers and whispered against her lips, "And I love you, Corrine. Always."

She kissed him softly before turning back on her

side, playing the little spoon to him. He watched Gabe move closer to her in sleep and nuzzle her neck. Braxas knew the road that lay ahead of them would not be easy, but he was more than ready to face it, to eradicate the danger from their lives, and finally give Corrine the happily ever after she so deserved.

Content at least for the moment, his heart full of love for his mate, overjoyed that she returned it, Braxas closed his eyes and fell into a deep and dreamless sleep. His peacefulness, however, was short-lived when he jerked awake just after dawn to find Corrine sitting upright in bed, her eyes glazed over.

"It has begun," she said in a voice that barely sounded like her own.

Gabe sat up as well looking just as concerned, but neither of them spoke for fear of disrupting Corrine's vision.

"What did you see, Corrine?" Gabe asked after her eyes had returned to normal.

She breathed heavy. "I saw blood and bits and pieces of shifters clawing at each other." She swallowed hard before continuing. "I heard growls and tearing of flesh. I don't…"

"What is it, love?" Braxas didn't like the look on her face. She seemed to be deciphering something that confused her, and he knew by now that though Corrine's visions weren't always so clear cut, they somehow made sense to her, as did the different paths that could possibly be taken.

"This vision felt a bit off to me," Corrine finally said. "My visions can change so quickly and with just a single course of action, which is probably why I usually get them in pieces or with symbols to show what *may* happen, and I've already proven that I am not infallible in deciphering their meaning." She waved off their concern. "I'm not dwelling on the past. I promise. It's just that normally I see what hasn't yet come to pass."

"So then why was this one so off for you?" Braxas asked.

"Because I think I saw something that had already happened or was happening at the time."

Gabe shot off the bed and began to dress as he asked, "What do you mean it already happened? What did you see?"

Braxas got up as well and held out his hand for Corrine to take. He tried to focus on the task of getting dressed, rather than the need to ravage his gorgeous and naked mate. He walked over to the dresser and picked up a matching yellow and white lace bra and panty set and a long white sundress with yellow daisies embroidered on the lower half of the dress.

Braxas quirked his brow. "Was this here last night?"

He handed the items to Corrine before turning back to the dresser. Next to where Corinne's items had just been, Braxas saw a pair of pants and a black V-neck t-shirt. Both looked to be his size.

Gabe had paused mid-dress and looked down at his clothes. "These aren't mine either, but damn if they aren't the perfect fit." He then slipped a long-sleeved, blue shirt over his head and prompted Corrine to continue.

"They must really like yellow here," he heard her mumble as she proceeded to dress in the mysteriously appeared items. "I doubt the girls snuck in here while we were sleeping, so it makes me wonder just how many more cool tricks they have up their sleeves." She shook her head.

Braxas walked over to her and helped her with

the clasp of her bra. She was shaking like a leaf, stalling, it seemed.

She took in another deep breath. "I saw glimpses of a hyena and a tiger. They were clawing at something and blood was spilling. I'm pretty sure it happened last night while we were sleeping."

"Whose blood, baby?" Gabe asked as he, too, came over to her. "And why do you think it already happened?"

"When I see the future, I feel weightless, almost like a ghost floating around, but this time my body felt heavy, *weighted* down like I was walking through something that would stay the course."

Braxas felt a sick twisting in his gut. "We've been away too long."

"Agreed," Gabe said.

The twisting inside Braxas turned to anger and then determination. "A single course of action can change an outcome," he said aloud.

"Yes," Corrine acknowledged.

"Where are you going with this?" Gabe asked, but he saw a gleam in his eyes, so in sync with the two of them, that Gabe must already have an inkling of what Braxas was about to say.

"If any of our people were hurt last night, swift justice will find the perpetrators," Braxas began, and both Gabe and Corrine nodded encouragingly, "but based on Corrine's previous vision and the fact that the three of us are here, last night was not the battle that Corrine foresaw all those years ago. I believe that whatever happened was only the beginning. From the chatter I have been hearing, the rogues were still recruiting. Perhaps, they had not succeeded in getting what they wanted last night, but I have no doubt that their end game is war."

"Then a war is what they will get," Gabe said through gritted teeth.

"Exactly." Braxas could feel the bloodthirsty grin split across his own face. "Only we are not going to wait around for them to finish gathering their army. We are not going to fight this war when the rogues deem fit to do so. If a single course of action can change an outcome, we're about to travel down a different road."

Gabe's face lit up in understanding. "If there's going to be a battle, it'll be fought on *our* terms this time."

Chapter Nineteen

They stepped out of the charming cabin and Corrine smiled, knowing that she would forever hold the sweet memories of their mating night here. She was surprised to see Aeron and Alak sitting atop the short stone wall that surrounded a small garden next to the cabin.

"Ah, refreshed and newly mated I see?" Alak smiled as he jumped down and held out a small basket that held some kind of breakfast pastries. "From some of the ladies to break your fast."

Corrine couldn't help the blush that rose to her cheeks as they looked at her. She could only assume the entire village knew what they'd gotten up to last night.

"Forgive my brother's teasing, Lady Corrine." Aeron threw Alak a dirty look and stood to lightly bow to her. "You've honored our people by letting our village host your mating night. May the Goddess grant you joy in all things and may your love burn forever bright."

"Thank you for your blessings, Aeron." Corrine took the basket and smiled back at him.

"We need to be on our way now, I'm afraid," Gabe said, taking Corrine's free hand in his own. "Thank you both for your hospitality. Are you still intending to accompany us back?"

"As the Goddess wills it, so shall it be done," Alak answered and turned to walk towards a path in the treeline. "Come, we will lead the way."

Gabe followed behind the Dark Fae, leading Corrine by the hand behind him. Braxas came next and then Alak. Corrine was just looking forward to being home once again now that she was mated. When she'd first realized that Braxas was also meant to be hers, she couldn't imagine how the Goddess could be so cruel. To give her two glorious mates, only to have them both be Alphas from different territories. She had thought it would be an impossible task to bring them together. The Goddess worked in mysterious ways indeed. Gabe and Braxas had surprised her with the strength of their love and determination to make their mating work no matter what. Corrine never imagined she would be so blessed.

About fifteen minutes into their journey, Alak called out to his brother. "Aeron, I think we are far enough from the village."

Aeron simply stopped and nodded. Then he closed his eyes and extended his hands out towards the ground. She felt a peculiar breeze move all around them and the strange tattoos on the Dark Fae's skin began to slowly move. For a second it seemed as though time stopped altogether, and then as suddenly as it had started, the wind stopped as Corrine blinked in disbelief when she recognized the portal through the Veil directly in front of them.

"What just happened?" Braxas whispered from behind her, pulling her closer to him.

"We are at the portal," Alak said shrugging and continuing to walk towards it. "Would you have rather wasted two days traveling?"

Gabe looked back at her, and she imagined he could tell from the shock on her face that she had no idea this kind of magic was possible.

"You mean to tell me that Ishaya could have spared us those days of madness, letting the poison in our blood almost destroy us all?" Gabe growled low, his wolf rising to the surface with his temper.

Alak met Gabe's angry face on, his own eyes narrowing. "We do not serve you, wolf."

The High Dorum stood his ground, not even

blinking in the wake of the furious Alpha, but his brother once again took a more diplomatic route, stepping forward.

"Ishaya does not wield these kinds of powers. They are gifted to only to a few of us in the service of our Goddess," Aeron calmly explained. "You traveled as you were meant to."

"What the hell is that supposed to mean?" Braxas chimed in, his grip on Corrine tightening. "Do you have any idea what we went through to get to you?"

"The Goddess Ryssana need not explain her motivations to you," Alak replied haughtily.

"For the love of the Goddess, Alak," Aeron sighed and rolled his eyes at his brother. "Stop taunting them."

Corrine could have sworn she saw Alak's mouth curve into a devious smile as he turned to walk towards the portal. He was a troublemaker. There was no doubt in her mind about that.

"Truly, all we can tell you is that there must have been a reason the Goddess sent you on your journey," Aeron explained. "Sometimes in life, the lessons are to be learned along your path and not at your destination."

Gabe and Braxas seemed to calm down at Aeron's explanation. She could feel their anger slowly recede along their link.

"Your brother is a dick," Gabe said before he grabbed Corrine's hand and pulled her along behind him, her mouth hanging open in shock.

"Gabe," she whispered, "you shouldn't speak to them like that. The Goddess can probably hear everything."

"Well, then she probably knows he's a dick, too," Braxas added in Gabe's defense as they approached where Alak was waiting for them.

"You won't hear me disagree with you, wolf," Aeron said with a smirk towards Alak's scowling face as both men raised their hands towards the portal and the gateway opened up.

Corrine exhaled loudly when they set foot back on the human side of the Veil. She was shocked when she realized that she now thought of this realm as home. This was where her mates were, where the rest of her pack and family were. A smile grew on her lips at that thought, and she squeezed the hands of the men she loved, causing them both to smile back.

"It smells odd here." Alak scrunched up his nose as if he'd just stepped downwind of an outhouse. "What *is* that?"

"Yes, there is a definite metallic taste to the air here," Aeron agreed.

"It's probably the pollution from machinery you can smell," Corrine said. She thought back to when she first crossed over all those years ago. "It took me some time to get used to it. I can't even notice it now."

Gabe took a deep breath. "That way is home," he said pointing in the direction of their property through the trees. "Come on. It's only a short walk to the house."

She watched the twins as they exited the woods and finally came to the edge of pack lands, their expressions guarded, but Corrine could tell some of what they saw surprised them. She had to stifle a giggle when they approached the driveway and Alak's hand went to his blade as if he expected the parked trucks to attack him.

"What are these beasts?" Aeron whispered to her, but he took his cue from the rest of the group, and since they weren't concerned, it seemed that he wasn't going to be either.

"The trucks?" Braxas asked, turning to look at him, "They aren't alive. They're machines we use to travel."

"Machines?" Alak went closer and poked one with the tip of his blade as if trying to make sure it wouldn't attack.

"Hey!" Gabe grumbled. "I just waxed that. You'll scratch the paint."

"Let's go inside and get you two settled," Corrine said taking Aeron's arm and leading him up the stairs to the back porch. "There will be plenty of new things to show you in the house, and I seriously need a bucket of coffee."

Donovan opened the door and met them as they approached, but the look on his face, however, told her that something was wrong.

"What's happened now?" Gabe sighed as he stepped past his Beta and led the rest of them into the kitchen.

"It's the cougars." Donovan looked at Braxas. "They were attacked by the rogues. Katrina called and she sent most of your people here, Braxas, but she said she was going to track their attackers."

"Fuck," the cougar growled. "Corrine's vision!"

Corrine couldn't remember seeing him so angry before. "Was anyone—"

"Katrina said there were a few injuries—one serious—but everyone survived," the wolf Beta continued. "April and Erica will heal them once they arrive. I tried to convince Katrina to come here first and wait for you, Braxas, but she's very … shit, well, she's stubborn as hell."

"Yes, I am aware of that," Braxas grumbled as he called his second. "Kat! Pick up the damned phone."

"I'm sure she's all right." Corrine tried to soothe

some of the worries she could feel coming from her mate. "And the rest of your pard is all right and on their way here to where it's safe."

"Yes," he sighed and pulled her in for a hug, "but Katrina had better stay out of trouble. We have no idea yet who we're really dealing with in all this mess. She's going to drive me crazy."

"We'll find her," Gabe added before turning back to his Beta. "Donovan, we'll need to make sure that all the cabins and bunkhouses are ready for the rest of the pard."

Corrine yawned, and kept her eyes closed for a moment, just enjoying her mate's embrace.

"Baby, you're tired." Braxas pulled back and gave her a gentle kiss. "Why don't you go on up and take a nap? We'll get Alak and Aeron settled in here."

"Are you sure?" She looked back at the twins, who were now rummaging through the fridge with fascinated expressions. "They're going to have a lot of questions, and you two didn't get much sleep either."

"We were the ones who kept you up, remember?" Gabe said, giving her a wink. "We will pay the consequences. Besides, we'll just make them some sandwiches, give them a case of beer, and set them in front of the TV. That's how you babysit men, darling."

"All right, if you say so," Corrine said. She laughed when Braxas gave her a swat on the ass as she passed by to get to the stairs.

"We'll come up and join you in a few hours, love," Gabe said with a smile. "Oh, and you may as well go to my room because that's where we'll be moving all of your things tomorrow."

"Is that right?" She gave him a saucy smile over her shoulder. "Do you think now that we're mated the

Goddess has performed a miracle and I'll do everything you say?"

"Nah, baby," Gabe replied right before he gave her a wink. "I'm just counting on your common sense to get my way. My bed's the only one big enough for the three of us."

****

Corrine opened her eyes and smiled as she stretched out and dual grunts sounded out on each side of her. It felt so good to be safe at home, snuggled in between the two men that she loved. She took a glance at the clock. *Yikes!* She'd been napping for more than four hours, and at this rate, she'd never sleep tonight.

"I'm going to go get something started for dinner," she said, getting out of bed quickly and deftly avoiding her mates' grasping arms which were trying to keep her in bed. While hunting for her clothes, she asked, "How were the guys doing when you left?"

"They accused us of using dark magic to spy on others when we put the hockey game on," Gabe grumbled, "but once we explained that the people knew they were being watched, they seemed to enjoy it."

Corrine dressed quickly then went downstairs to see how her guests were adjusting to being on this side of the Veil. She stopped abruptly when she came into the living room and found them engrossed by the television, scattered empty food packages littered all around them.

"Have you guys been watching TV this entire time?"

"Lady Corrine!" Aeron stood, a look of relief on his face. "We're so glad you're back. After studying your people on the viewing crystal we are concerned."

"Indeed, this Mother of Dragons could be quite a powerful adversary." Alak didn't take his eyes off of the blonde woman on the television. "Does your pack have an alliance with her? If not, we need to come up with some spells that would work against the kind of beasts she controls."

Corrine tried to keep the smile off her face as she picked up the remote and turned off the *Game of Thrones* marathon that had them so worked up.

This is exactly the kind of thing that happens when you leave men to babysit.

Chapter Twenty

"I am telling you, brother, there is magic involved in this," Gabe heard one of the twins say in the main living room. Gabe stepped silently from the stairs he'd just walked down and stood by the door. Because the two bastards sounded exactly the same, Gabe had no clue which one had spoken.

"You have said that about everything we have encountered since we stepped through the Veil," the other one answered with a patient note to his tone, and Gabe was willing to be money that it was Aeron.

"But this goes beyond everything that we have seen so far, Aeron."

Ding, ding, ding!

"How are they able to speak to other people through those small metal devices?" Aeron continued. "I heard Lady Corrine talking with the mate of the large dark-haired male, Donovan, and when I asked where this woman, April was, Corrine said in a store called 'Cost-co' that is over an hour away from here in one of their mechanical beasts! They have no telepathic skills, so how is this possible?"

Gabe stepped into the room with a grin he knew could be described as shit-eating. "It's called a phone, oh exalted one, who can travel from one destination to another in the space of a second. We'll hook you up with a cell phone and an internet connection so you can Google this shit and get the answers. Hell, I've even heard of people Googling themselves to see what turns up!"

Both men scowled at him, and Gabe saw Alak's sword hand twitch.

Alak growled. "I do not wish for this internet connection to do the Googling on me. I do not think the

Goddess would approve."

Gabe threw his head back and roared with laughter. "Fuck me, I don't remember Corrine being so quick to leap for the sword every time she encountered anything new. Must be that male insecurity shit she is always accusing me of."

Donovan stepped into the room, a quizzical look on his face, no doubt put there because Gabe was not one to laugh out loud much. "Alpha, your mates are waiting for you in the kitchen. The rest of your council members are on their way, and Braxas is reaching out to the senior members of his pard, as well." Donovan rubbed his hands with glee. "I do so love a little wartime planning as a starter to a meal."

Gabe was still grinning like an idiot when he stepped into the kitchen, Aeron and Alak right behind him. His heart swelled at the sight of his woman standing at the stove, and he walked straight to her, pressing against her back, and placing an open-mouthed kiss against his claiming bite. Fuck, it did something visceral to him seeing his mate wearing his mark.

"About time you got your lazy ass outta bed, Gabe. Braxas has been down for a half hour helping," Corrine murmured as she replaced the lid to the pot she had finished adding stuff to.

Gabe growled against the soft skin of her neck and delighted in the shiver of awareness he felt roll through her. "If I'd been able to convince you to stay, I bet Braxas wouldn't have been so damn keen to get downstairs."

"Hell no," Braxas said from where he leaned back against the kitchen island. "Nothing would have gotten me out of that bed."

Gabe turned to his friend, because despite his

words, there was something in his tone that had Gabe's wolf standing alert. The look on Braxas's face was not as relaxed as his posture and body language might have implied, and Gabe knew exactly why the large man was on edge.

"Still nothing from Katrina?"

Braxas frowned and the worry he had been hiding became clear on his face. "No, nothing."

Corrine pulled away from him, and Gabe let her walk toward Braxas. When she got to him, she pressed herself into him, knowing exactly what the cougar needed. Braxas seemed to sigh in relief as he wrapped his arms around her and rubbed his cheek against her. "And that is so unlike her. Katrina is a badass, and I know she knows how to look after herself. Hell, she's my second for a reason. But she always, *always* checks in with me when she is on a mission."

"You send your women into battle?" Alak asked, judgment clear in his tone, which was immediately followed by the growl of an unhappy wolf meshed with the rumble of a displeased cougar.

"There are many fierce women here who would be insulted by that question," Braxas said in a voice slightly garbled, an indication that his animal hovered just below the surface. "In our world, we all fight to protect our own equally, and no one fights harder for my people than Katrina."

"Forgive my brother, Braxas." Aeron stepped forward, shooting a look at Alak that had him stepping back and holding up a hand in surrender, but Gabe noticed the big bastard didn't offer a word of apology. "We of all people know that women are strong. We only have to look at our Goddess, and the examples of our women who fight by their men," Aeron said, indicating Corrine with a flick of his jaw and a smile. "But, there are those among us, like my brother, who are somewhat overprotective in their views of the fairer sex."

Corrine turned in Braxas's arms and leaned back against him, leveling Alak with a look that Gabe knew only too well. "You do your Goddess a dishonor by acting like a jerk. And if you need a translation for that…"

Alak shook his head. "No, Lady Corrine, I do not require a translation."

Corrine held the Fae's gaze for a long moment, and Gabe couldn't hold back the grin when the man appeared to fidget slightly. "Good, now come to the table, and leave your weapons at the door."

Both Alak and Aeron looked unsettled by the request but removed their swords.

"At least we don't have to worry about Alak taking out the damn toaster or something," Donovan said with a grin.

Alak frowned, and Gabe knew it was because he desperately wanted to ask what a toaster was, but didn't want to admit that he didn't know in the first place.

Corrine, Braxas, and a few others loaded the table with food. As the men and women, wolves and cougars, all descended on the kitchen to gather a plate and fill it with food, Gabe felt a warmth spread within him. This was what it was to be a pack. He shot a quick glance at Braxas and saw a similar look of pride on the man's face. Gabe figured this was what it meant to be a pard as well. Either way, pack or pard, this was family.

They had just finished eating when Braxas's phone rang. When he pulled it from his pocket, Gabe snorted a laugh when he saw Alak look at it warily. He would have thrown a smart-ass comment in the Fae's direction, but Braxas's first words had Gabe listening in to the conversation, all thought of hassling the Fae gone.

"Katrina, I swear to God, you will be the death of me," Braxas growled into the phone, but the relief was clear in his tone. Unfortunately, it was short-lived.

Instead of Katrina, he—and naturally, the other shifters in the room as well—heard a male's voice answer. "How apt," the voice said. "I am not your bitch Katrina, but by the will of the fucking Gods, I *will* be the death of you."

Gabe's wolf growled menacingly within him, the sound vibrating through his chest. He recognized that voice, as he knew that Braxas did as well. It belonged to Nyx Santini, a hyena shifter with questionable moral fiber as well as personal hygiene. Unfortunately, that was about as positive as it came for Nyx.

"Santini," Braxas growled pulling the phone away and pressing it onto speaker for those without the benefit of enhanced hearing from their shifter genes. "If you've got my second's phone, then I am guessing you are bleeding. You might want to get to the reason for your call before you pass the fuck out."

A laugh came from the phone. "Oh, there was bloodshed, I can assure you of that, but your little pussy didn't cut me as much as we did her."

Gabe saw a muscle in Braxas's jaw tick as his dominance began to slowly fill the room. "But she did bleed you," he persisted, his voice calm despite the rage Gabe could feel rolling off him, "and for that, I will reward her greatly when she is back with the pard. Now, be a good little sociopath and tell me to what do I owe the pleasure of this conversation."

"So fucking confident," Nyx spat down the phone, and there was no mistaking the man's hatred. "You and that fucking dog Alpha think you are superior to the rest of us. Well, we heard about your little fuck triangle with the Fae whore, and figured we'd be rude not to celebrate the occasion with a little get-together of our own."

Gabe growled low, the room now filling with his own dominance, and from the way his pack and Braxas's pard all scowled and tilted their heads, the pressure was building exponentially. "Get to the point, prick," Gabe spat, his voice practically throbbing with rage. "Or simply tell us where to find you and we can come continue this conversation face to face. I have a little something in mind for you as well for daring to disrespect my mate."

"In *my* time, dog, not yours," Nyx growled in response. "Speak again and I will put another bullet in the cat bitch." Gabe fought the urge to threaten the asshole some more. "Do you want your second back, Braxas? Then come get her. Alone. We see any of your pard or the dog's pack, then we will skin the bitch alive and leave her for you to find … maybe after some of my men have had a little taste of her first. I will send you the coordinates. Be there at noon tomorrow. Hmmm, how *shall* we pass the time?"

Just before the phone was disconnected, they heard a woman scream in pain. All color drained from Braxas's face, and Gabe shot forward with all the speed he could muster and pulled the phone from his hand before Braxas could crush it.

"Calm, brother," Gabe said as he held Braxas's gaze, pulling Corrine between them, using the power of their mated triad to calm the man and the cougar within him. "We will get our pack-mate back." There was a quick inhalation from those in the room as Gabe claimed Katrina and the rest of Braxas's people in that sentence.

"That we will," Braxas agreed, the color slowly

returning to his skin, but his eyes still blazing with hatred. "Our pard and our pack will never turn their back on family."

Gabe nodded as Braxas returned the claim.

"We'll get her back, and we'll dine on the hearts of the fuckers who dared take her," Gabe promised. "I have a plan, and as always, it is fucking brilliant."

Gabe's grin was bloodthirsty as he turned to point at the two large Fae who stood stoically at the side of the room. "And it involves the two of you."

Chapter Twenty-One

Braxas stepped out of the woods and into a circular clearing—the exact coordinates dictated to him by Nyx. It looked as if a fire had ravaged this barren space, located deep in the thick of the forest.

He heard movement through the trees in front of him before he saw them. Nyx Santini stepped out, flanked by six other shifters, three on each side of him, and he looked every bit as arrogant as Braxas remembered from their last not so pleasant encounter. His light brown, chin length hair now had blond highlights in it, and it appeared that Santini had finally managed to sprout a decent looking beard and gained some heavy artillery in the form of muscles. His unbuttoned shirt revealed it all.

What a douche, Braxas thought to himself. That guy had always been hotheaded and only a little brighter than the dumbest tool in the shed.

The hyena pack Nyx had once belonged to often liked to tangle with Braxas's pard until he, with Gabe's help, had put a stop to it years ago. Together, they took out the power hungry Alpha of the pack, who was later replaced by someone a good deal more tolerable. Nyx, who had been their Beta, deserted his people. It was no wonder he had a grudge against both Braxas and Gabe, but Braxas knew there had to be far more to his building an army of Rogues than to start a war with two of the most powerful packs in all of North America. Nyx lacked the Alpha gene, and Braxas remembered that he had made a very poor choice as a Beta. There was no way a large group of shifters would follow him indefinitely.

"You wanted me?" Braxas asked. He then spread out his arms, palms open, like humans envisioned Jesus doing on a cross. "Here I am. Now where is Katrina?"

"You have a choice here today," replied a familiar voice *behind* Nyx. In seconds, more shifters emerged through the trees, all but the voice that spoke, and they began to slowly surround him on all sides, some moving behind him, until finally, the male behind the voice he knew so well showed himself.

Braxas sneered as a surge of hatred for this man filled him. He should have known who would be behind all of this. "I'd say it's good to see you, cousin, but it would be more apt to say I hoped that you'd have been dead by now."

His cousin, Zayden Beaumont, shook his head as his rogues stared back and forth at them in shock. Apparently, their fearless leader had not been completely forthcoming with them about his familial ties.

Just then, another rogue stepped out from behind the trees and said, "I searched the perimeter. He came alone."

Satisfied, Zayden turned to Braxas. "Now is that any way to greet your own flesh and blood?" he tsked.

"You never said he was your cousin," Nyx griped from beside him. He then narrowed his eyes at Zayden in suspicion.

"It's of no consequence to our arrangement, Nyx," Zayden said. He turned and faced the hyena and placed a hand on his shoulder. "We have a trust built between us, you and I and our men." He waited until Nyx nodded and relaxed his features before turning back to Braxas. "Yes, Braxas *Beaumont* is indeed my cousin," he announced to his men all the while keeping his gaze firmly locked on Braxas, "but we shall finally discover here today if blood will be enough to lead him down the right path. If he will join our righteous cause or—"

"Righteous cause?" Braxas threw his head back

and barked out a sarcastic laugh. "Is this the bullshit you feed these men? I look around at these faces and see some good men, some I have met before, some of whom have lost during battles and have been displaced. Your offer to them is to be ruled under your thumb on your quest for power. I know better than anyone that power is what you have always sought."

Braxas caught the flicker of Zayden's composed façade falter. He doubted that anyone else even picked up on it, but then again, none of these men, probably not even Nyx, the man who appeared to be his second, knew him like Braxas did. They had, after all, been close once, especially being that their fathers were brothers. Braxas's father had been the Alpha of the cougars, Zayden's, the Beta, and even though it was always known that Braxas would be the one to succeed his father, there never seemed to be any jealousy between the two. Zayden had just always assumed that he would become the Beta, despite being a tiger shifter—his mother's gene had been the prevalent one from a mixed mating.

The type of shifter Zayden turned out to be had no bearing on his position of becoming Beta. It was his desire to control, his perception of himself as being above others, and his lack of fair judgment that Braxas began to notice as they got older. After the battle that killed both of their fathers, Zayden became relentless in pursuing anyone he deemed a future threat, ruthless even. On the day that Braxas had chosen Katrina to be his second, Zayden challenged him. In the end, wounded, prideful, even though Braxas conceded to allow him to remain with the pack, Zayden walked away, never to be seen or heard from by Braxas until today.

Braxas was actually glad that this day had come. Years after Zayden's departure from the pack, Braxas had discovered that his own cousin had been the one to incite the war that caused the death of their fathers. He had been thirsting for a moment like this, although when he had pictured it, the only casualty had been Zayden himself.

Unfortunately, as he looked at the faces of the rogues dispersed around him, he could tell they would fight for Zayden to the death.

"What I sought," Zayden began matter-of-factly, "was my rightful place ... by *your* side, I might add. You chose the little pussy over your own blood, and look at where she ended up."

"With her claw marks still on you," Braxas said with a snarl. He smiled as he stared at the fresh marks across Zayden's neck. He could tell from the fact that it wasn't healed yet that Katrina had delivered them recently, which also meant that she wasn't too far away. He tilted his head to the side slightly, a signal that would be completely imperceptible to the men who stood in front of him. "She has proven her worth as my second a million times over, cousin. I do not regret my choice, especially seeing what you are trying to do here, and what you *did* do all those years ago."

Zayden pursed his lips and narrowed his eyes. The rogues stared back and forth between them again. At least they all knew for certain now that the so-called trust Zayden spoke of was only one-sided.

"Did you think I wouldn't find out that the war that killed our fathers was instigated by you?" Braxas spat.

"I did what I thought was nec—"

"You did what you thought was best for *you*, and it cost us our fathers!" Braxas roared. "Now, you wanted me. I'm here. Release Katrina. Or do you want these men to see that you are not a man of your word?"

All eyes were now on Zayden, and Braxas could see the flare of rage in the man's eyes at having his word questioned. He knew that the bastard had something up his sleeve, and it didn't surprise him in the least that this wasn't going to be as simple as an exchange. Not that he was planning for it to be anyway.

"I have no intention of going back on anything," Zayden replied, sounding cool and collected once again. "Nyx couldn't very well give you the specifics over the phone and that would have ruined seeing the surprised look on your face for me, but I fully intend to lay it all out for you now." Zayden and Nyx took a few steps forward. "As I stated earlier, you have a choice to make. Your little bitch will go free, provided you join us. Swear fealty to me, cousin, and the quarrel between us shall be forgotten."

Braxas felt his lip curl in disgust. "We have far more than a quarrel between us."

"There is more to my generous offer," Zayden continued as if Braxas had not spoken. "I heard you were newly mated, and I offer you my congratulations and my help in getting rid of the dog for you. Why share what you can have all to yourself?"

Braxas curled his hands into fists at his sides. Zayden couldn't possibly think that he would agree to this, Braxas thought, and he wondered at first if he'd simply brought him out here to kill him. However, as Braxas stared at his demented cousin, he saw a glimmer of hope in the other man's eyes. Zayden may actually *want* his fealty after all. It would certainly repair the damage that Braxas had done to his pride, and to have Braxas serve underneath him would be an even bigger ego boost.

The words "Kneel before Zod" rolled through

Braxas's mind as Zayden's motivation, at least in part, dawned on him. He almost felt sorry for his cousin … almost. Zayden had a lot to answer for, a debt that would take more than one lifetime to pay. His father and uncle's death, capturing and hurting Katrina, and now threatening to kill one-third of his triad—these sins he would bleed for.

"And my other option is?"

"Death," Zayden answered simply with a shrug of his shoulders.

"I choose death then," Braxas snarled as his claws extended. "Yours!"

Braxas's shirt ripped down the center as he quickly turned a half shift. The rogues surrounding him looked between Zayden and Braxas yet again, uncertain of what to do, it seemed. Zayden stood his ground smugly as did Nyx beside him, until the ground beneath them began to shake. Braxas gave his cousin and Nyx a bloodthirsty smile as their confident demeanor was suddenly replaced with fear. Their fear only grew when Braxas noticed one of the shifters in his right peripheral vision was lifted by an unseen force and thrown hard against a tree. The rest of the rogues looked wildly around for the source, but Braxas only had eyes for his cousin.

With a roar, Braxas charged Zayden, and like a curtain lifted, an army of wolves and cougars appeared seemingly out of nowhere. Just as the rogues had been surrounding Braxas, his entire pack had been surrounding them, the audience to everything that had just played out. The two very talented High Dorum twins had cloaked them, not just from view, but from senses as well. Gabe's plan had been brilliant.

He also knew that Corrine would not be left out of it, nor would he ask that of her. He had fought beside her in the war against the False King of the Fae and knew how fierce she could be in battle. That's why he could think of no one better to put his trust in to save his Beta. He had seen Corrine nod her understanding to his signal, as the twins did not shield anything from him, and he had seen her leave with Erica and April in tow.

Based on the arrogance he had witnessed rolling off of the tiger and hyena, he'd hoped that they would not see the need to keep Katrina under heavy guard while they were assembled here with him. In any case, he'd seen firsthand what Erica was capable of with her powers and heard that April, though still in training with a blade, packed a pretty powerful punch with her similar gifts. He had yet to get to know this woman, who was the niece of his beloved, and now his by extension.

Zayden had done a half shift by the time Braxas had collided with him. Braxas tore into his flesh, determined not to simply wound his cousin this time. As he turned to get a swipe in on Nyx, the hyena had no longer been near him. Instead, he found him deep in battle with Gabe. The ground continued to shake underneath them, but Braxas's footing felt completely steady. He understood now what Gabe had told him about Frederych's powers, how Gabe and the wolves not only battled the Fae, but Mother Nature as well, only this time, Mother Nature was *their* ally.

Braxas growled as Zayden sank his sharp claws in his shoulder. His cousin's skill as a fighter had greatly improved. Perhaps he had underestimated him as well, a mistake Braxas would not repeat. He sharpened his focus on his enemy, both men tearing into each other with ferocity. Braxas retracted the claws from his right hand to punch Zayden repeatedly, and his canines dropped with the urge to draw blood. He went for it, sinking his sharp teeth into the tiger's forearm as he blocked against another strike.

Zayden yelled from pain, and anger overtook his earlier coolness completely due to his pride being once again trampled on. He may have acquired more skills in battle, but Braxas was still the better warrior. As further proof, Braxas struck him again and again, blocking every blow that Zayden threw at him. Just when Zayden's smugness would return, Braxas would dodge another seemingly unavoidable hit. He flipped backward, kicking Zayden in the face, and before he even had time to regain his senses, Braxas swept his feet out from under him.

He had him. Zayden was his, awaiting the final death strike, one that Braxas would have successfully delivered had it not been for the anguished scream he heard coming from Corrine.

"Gabe!"

Chapter Twenty-Two

Corrine had taken the cue from Braxas and snuck away with Erica and April to go and find Katrina, hoping that the guys had been correct in thinking the bulk of the rogue forces would be drawn to the confrontation, giving the girls an opportunity to strike.

When they finally came upon the dark SUV, it was only being guarded by one shifter, whom Erica easily knocked out and left unconscious on the ground. Corrine tried not to look shaken when they opened up the rear hatch and saw Katrina gagged and tied up, dried blood covering her mouth and neck. The shirt she wore was covered as well and that should have been the most shocking part, but damn, the expression she wore was more than a bit scary. That was one pissed off cat. If looks could kill, then she had no doubt that every one of the rogues would have been six feet under already. When Erica removed the gag, a litany of mumbled curse words Corrine had never even heard before came out of the beautiful blonde woman.

"Fuck," Kat finally spat out. Her lower split lip still bled profusely, which puzzled Corrine. Even if it had happened fairly recently, the wound should have begun to clot by now. "Where is Braxas? I need to tell him this is a trap by his asshole cousin. He should never have agreed to come for me."

"We assumed it was a trap," Erica answered, frowning at the strange metallic cuffs holding Kat's wrists. "Braxas is fine, and he isn't alone out there. Don't move for a second. What are these cuffs? They have Fae writing on them."

"I don't know." Kat scowled down at the metal. "They don't allow me to shift any part of myself, though, and I was unable to remove them."

"Where in the hell did the rogues get these from?" Erica fiddled with them some more before finally they popped open and dropped to the ground. She picked them up and stuffed them in her pocket.

"They look like the ones that were used on Jason in the palace dungeons," April said, her voice angry. She then turned to Katrina. "Are you okay? Is all that blood yours?" Corrine looked concerned as well when she took in the sight of the various bruises and cuts still marring Katrina's golden skin as well as the rips in her blood-soaked clothing, "Those bastards didn't … umm…"

Corrine couldn't blame her niece for having a hard time voicing the words that no doubt they had all been thinking. When Kat shook her head in denial, Corrine let out the breath she'd been holding.

"Most of it isn't my blood, and only one of Nyx's buddies tried anything before they got the cuffs on me," Kat added, "but I made sure to make an example of him. Just an FYI, shifters can't re-grow limbs once they've been ripped off. Not all of the men with Zayden and Nyx are bad. I think they just don't see that they have another option, but once the cuffs were put on, a few of the rogues made sure to take turns guarding me, keeping some of their more unsavory members at bay."

"That's a relief. Sweet Goddess, Kat, you're covered in blood," Erica said, still looking concerned. "Do you need us to heal anything before we get back to the group?"

"I think I'll be fine now." The cuts were already beginning to form scabs since she'd been released from the strange handcuffs.

Corrine was impressed by her mate's second. Katrina was quite a force to be reckoned with. Though she looked like hell, her face swollen and bruised, covered in the blood of her enemies, the fire in her eyes revealed that she was eager as ever to join in the battle and protect her Alpha.

"Will there be more rogues coming back?" April asked as they tied up the unconscious guard and placed him in the back of the vehicle where Kat had been.

"No, that arrogant fuck, Zayden, wanted them all to go with him to the meet, no doubt thinking it would make him look more impressive than he actually is." Kat opened the passenger side front door and seemed to be looking for something in the glove box, cursing when she came up empty. "Un-fucking-believable little rat."

"What?" Corrine was concerned at the look of worry that was now all over Katrina's face.

"That sociopath Nyx took his toy with him," she muttered. "He's got some sick fascination with cutting people. I'd hoped he left it behind to fight with some honor like a real shifter would, but I guess I should have known better."

Her words sank in, and suddenly Corrine felt like a huge claw was tightening around her heart. Something was about to go wrong—it was a feeling this time, not a vision. She needed to get to her mates.

"We need to go, now!" She turned and started running towards the clearing, desperate panic welling in every cell in her body. Her instincts kept screaming at her.

When they broke from the cover of the forest, they arrived smack dab in the middle of a full-on battle. Half of the field was full of fighting shifters, while the others fought in human form or frightening half-shifted ones. Braxas was easy to spot since it was tough to miss two giant cat men trading blows—one a mass of golden fur, and the other head to toe in the black and orange tiger stripes, and both were also covered in a liberal amount of blood.

Luckily Braxas seemed to have the upper hand. He'd just knocked Zayden on his ass, going in for the kill, when Corrine's eyes finally found her other mate. Gabe was fighting with a wiry, crazed looking Nyx. Gabe had just delivered two long swipes with his claws across his opponent's chest, causing the other man to yelp and drop his arms to protect his wounds. As her mate wrapped his hand around the other man's neck and lifted him off the ground, she noticed something in Nyx's hand glint in the fading afternoon sun. She'd never seen shifters use weapons when they fought each other for any kind of pack dominance issues. It was an unspoken rule, but one *most* of them took very seriously. If a shifter couldn't defeat his rival with claws and teeth alone, then they didn't deserve the position they were fighting for. Corrine saw Nyx's arm jerk forward twice. The look of shock crossed her mate's face right before she screamed out and ran towards him.

"Gabe!"

Her vision narrowed until the only thing she could see was him. She was vaguely aware of the women around her fighting to clear a path for her, and she heard Braxas yell out for Gabe as well. He was closer than she was, and she couldn't have loved him more than when he left Zayden lying on the ground to rush to Gabe's side. Before Nyx's arm could swing back for another blow with the knife, Braxas was there. A loud crack of bone rang out as he grabbed the hyena's wrist and snapped it straight up before throwing him back to land a few feet away.

Goddess, there is so much blood. She dropped down beside her two men. Braxas had his hands covering the wounds, but the blood was freely flowing all around his fingers.

"Corrine, are you all right?" Gabe's voice was strained as he appeared to be searching her for any damage.

"Me? Sweet Goddess, Gabe, what did he do to you?" she cried. Erica and April pushed their way in to sit beside Gabe, moving everyone's hands away so they could begin healing him.

"That fucking rat-bastard stabbed me!" he yelled in disbelief. "I can't believe it."

The scene had gathered quite a crowd. It seemed as though many of the rogues stopped fighting when they realized what one of their leaders had done.

"They ran," Donovan shouted as he and Jason rushed over to them, covered in their own battle wounds. "We can't find Nyx or Zayden anywhere. They fled and left the rest of their men behind."

"Damn it, stop moving, Gabe," Erica cursed when he tried to sit up.

"Donovan, you take Ben and Leo and do a sweep of the woods to see if they're still out there," Braxas said in full command mode. He pushed Gabe back down and held him still. "Jason, maybe Alak and Aeron can help you get the rest of these rogues loaded up and taken back to the house so we can figure out what to do with them.

"I can search for Zayden," Katrina said. She seemed impatient and even more agitated than she had been when they'd rescued her. She kept stealing glances towards Aeron and Alak, perhaps trying to figure out who or what they were, Corrine thought.

"No, Kat, you're coming back with us." Braxas cut her off just when it seemed she was about to argue with him. "I need to take care of my mates, and I need you to have my back."

"Will he be all right?" Corrine asked. She was so thankful that Erica and April were here to heal Gabe's wounds.

"He should be, but he's lost a lot of blood." The serious look in Erica's eyes as she answered Corrine said volumes. If fate hadn't brought all of them together the way it had in the last few months, Gabe would have been a casualty of this battle, just the way Corrine had witnessed in her original vision.

****

Corrine watched Gabe carefully as they all made their way back to the trucks to go home. He said he was all patched up, but he was still moving rather slowly. This moment seemed almost anti-climactic—her vision of Gabe's death had haunted her daily for years—but she wasn't about to complain. She felt like the weight of a freight train had been lifted from her heart since the day she began waiting for the fates to take him away from her.

Aeron and Alak had made their job of transporting the captured rogues ridiculously easy, opening a portal straight back to their property, taking them all in two trips. But they'd returned for some reason, leaving Jason in charge back at the house.

"Kat, you drive my truck," Braxas directed as he and Corrine helped Gabe into the back seat of the other truck. "The twins can come with us."

"I don't even know these two," Katrina argued, gesturing at the Dark Fae, who were staring back at her rather intently. "I don't like them having access to you while you're distracted, Braxas. I should go with you instead."

"Do you think we would harm them?" Alak asked her, his eyes narrowing. "We are here to assist your people. You dare question our honor?"

Everyone just watched as Katrina took a step closer to him. It was like watching in slow motion an accident about to happen, but not being able to stop it, the tension between them palpable.

"Look, Gray and Grayer," she spat out, "I don't know you from a hole in the wall and it's my job to protect my Alpha. Plus, you've been staring at me since the battle ended, and I—don't—like—it." Katrina used her finger to poke out the last four words on Alak's chest and Aeron finally stepped up to intervene just as his brother was taking a deep breath to no doubt, issue a rebuttal.

"Forgive us, Lady Katrina." Aeron gently took her hand and held it, which seemed to stupefy Kat. She just looked at their joined hands like she didn't know what was happening. "We are simply overwhelmed by your golden beauty."

Corrine had to give Braxas an elbow in the ribs when his loud snort was heard by everyone. *Fucking men—didn't they ever have a clue?*

"We are overwhelmed by something, to be sure, but I'm not convinced she isn't using some kind of dark magic to ensnare us," Alak said.

Corrine rolled her eyes as Alak just couldn't keep his mouth shut while his brother tried to smooth things over with the temperamental shifter female.

"Why, you ... arrogant son of a bitch! Like I would ever need a fucking magic spell to turn your head!" Kat roared out and turned to storm back to the other truck, leaving Aeron's mouth hanging open in shock before he turned on his brother and punched him right in the face.

"Oh, my." Corrine didn't quite know what to say when Alak just shrugged and came back over to them, his pissed off twin trailing in his wake. "Umm, everyone back to the house I guess?"

"Yes, love," Gabe said sounding exhausted. He settled himself in the back seat, Aeron getting in on one side and Corrine beside him on the other.

Alak sat up front on the passenger's side. He placed his hand on the window, a small glow emitting from his palms. Seconds later, the window lowered just as Braxas started up the car. When they began to move, Alak stuck his head out of the window, making Corrine shake her head and chuckle. He reminded her of a golden retriever just then. All that was missing was him letting his tongue hang out.

They were only about twenty minutes into their drive when Gabe suddenly let loose a string of profanities. Startled, she turned to look at him. He was holding his stomach with a look of pure shock on his face. Then she noticed the bloom of bright red blood on the white t-shirt he'd put on after Erica had healed him— there was so much blood!

"Gabe, what's wrong? What's happening?" Corrine cried out, causing Braxas to hit the brakes and pull over.

Aeron leaned in closer to Gabe, hovering his hand over the wounds that wouldn't stop bleeding. His eyes met hers, and the concern she saw in them scared the hell out of her.

"There is dark magic in his wounds," Aeron explained. "These were made with no ordinary blade."

Chapter Twenty-Three

Gabe ignored the shouting around him and concentrated on his breathing, willing his body to accept the pain in his stomach. Someone had opened the door beside him, and he gratefully turned his face into the fresh air. He could hear his mate calling his name, but he needed to focus on trying to block out some of the pain. He took a couple of deep breaths, waiting until the urge to pass out abated slightly.

"It's all right, baby," Gabe murmured. "I'm still here."

"You're here, but you're bleeding badly," Corrine said, and there was no mistaking the quiver of fear in her tone. He would have done anything to try to assuage her anxiety, but truth be told, he could feel his own blood flowing freely over his hands still pressed to the wound. The amount was horrifying as was the cold that was beginning to overtake him.

"Fix this," he heard Braxas growl. "You two are both some kind of uber-talented fucking Fae. You need to fix this."

Gabe looked up at Aeron and Alak in time to see them share a wary look. "You can't?" Gabe asked quietly as both men turned to look at him. "Can you?"

Aeron winced and shook his head. "We do not think that this is for us to heal. If we were to try, we might end up killing you. The only thing that would work in our favor, would be if there were a bond between us. Without one, there is no connection to the light for us to follow. You will continue to fall into darkness, and you would take us with you."

Alak stepped forward. "There is only one who can save you, Gabe Erikkson, and that is your mate."

Gabe heard Corrine gasp, and he turned to look at her and had to fight the wave of nausea that washed over him at the move. His mate looked at him then back at the Dark Fae, her beautiful face a sea of fear and confusion.

"How can I do that?" Corrine whispered. "My powers are not to heal. Should we call for Erica or April?"

But Alak was already shaking his head. "Not you, Lady Corrine." And when he turned to his left to look right at Braxas, the look on the cougar's face mirrored the shock that filled Gabe.

"What?" Braxas gestured between himself and Gabe, looking confused. "Gabe and I share Corrine, not each other."

Braxas was firm in his response, but there was also a note of regret that he would be unable to save Gabe. Gabe would have seconded what Braxas had said and also would have tried to ease his guilt had he not been slammed with a jolt of pain. He groaned as a fresh wave of blood flowed over his fingers.

"Gabe!" Corrine cried out, and somehow he ended up in her arms, lying back on the seat with his legs out the door and his head in her lap.

"Shh, baby," he whispered. He had never felt so weak. "Listen to me. You are the best damn thing that has ever happened in my life. If I'm to die today, I—"

"No," Corrine sobbed, and Gabe could feel the heat of her tears against her skin as she leaned low to press her face against his. "I can't lose you, my love, not now, not after everything we have been through. This was not supposed to happen. Everything I did was to avoid this."

Gabe wanted to reach his hand up to cup her face and tell her that everything was going to be okay, but he simply lacked the strength. He remained still, looking up at his mate. If he were about to leave this life, then the last thing he wanted to see before he closed his eyes for the last time was Corrine's beautiful face.

****

"Fuck!" Braxas roared as he watched the poignant scene unfold before him. He could feel Corrine's devastation down their bond, and he didn't need to be completely connected to the wolf to know how he felt about it. The loss on his face was palpable.

He turned to Alak who stood beside him, grabbed him by his shirt, and slammed him against the car. With a low growl, he held him there with his arm across Alak's chest. "You have five seconds to explain. What the fuck do I have to do to save him?"

Braxas could see that Alak did not like being held like that, and something moved in the Dark Fae's eyes that he figured meant Alak was pissed, but Braxas didn't give a fuck. He held the man's gaze and waited, counting to three in his head. He got to the count of four when Alak spoke.

"You must claim the Alpha as you have claimed your woman."

Braxas jerked back. Did he really mean he had to take Gabe, as in a sexual way then bite him? Because he wasn't so sure he could do that. He had already developed a strong bond and love for Gabe, but it just wasn't sexual. It wasn't in his nature to be sexual with another man even though he found all forms of love beautiful. He knew the same to be true of Gabe.

"No," Alak continued with an exasperated tone in his voice, "I do not mean whilst in the sexual act of claiming. You are cementing the bond between two Alphas and their chosen mate, not claiming him as your own."

Aeron stepped closer. "There is a belief among our people that when two men of equal strength, take and claim a woman that connects them as nothing else could, then the bond of three may occur. Think of it like this. You have a bond with your mate, one that is connected by the fates and through her blood. The fates have deemed you and Gabe as worthy of the woman destined to be yours. To complete the circle, you need to connect through blood as well. Once it is completed, then the strength of that bond will lead to a rise in the physical enhancements that come with being an Alpha shifter."

"So I just have to bite him?"

Aeron nodded. "Yes, you must take of his blood, and he will need to take of yours. Then the circle will be complete. The poison from that blade wound will not take hold within you as long as that circle is completed."

"You have felt a growing emotional connection to the wolf, yes?" Alak asked.

Braxas nodded, looking at Gabe's limp body. He had even admitted as much to his pard and Gabe's pack. They were connected through the bond they both shared with Corrine, but it was more than that. They were brothers in every way now except for blood.

He stepped closer to Gabe, and Corrine's head snapped up with a fierce look on her face. Her expression told Braxas she would guard her mate viciously. His love for her swelled.

"It's okay, mate," Braxas said gently. "I understand now, and there is a way for me to help Gabe." Hope filled Corrine's expression.

Braxas took Gabe's arm in his and slid the blood-soaked sleeve of his shirt out of his way. With no hesitation, he bent and bit deep into Gabe's wrist. He caught the bitter tang of the poison that was affecting his friend so badly but didn't stop until he felt a connection snap into place within himself. When he pulled back, he half shifted his left hand, and drew four deep scratches across Gabe's forearm just above the bite make he'd just made.

"Help him to sit up, love," Braxas told Corrine and smiled when she hurried to comply. When he was sitting up, Braxas held his own wrist in front of Gabe, but frowned when he realized Gabe was practically unconscious. "How the hell am I going to get him to bite me back?"

No sooner had he asked that when an arm swung past him and his jaw dropped with shock as a fist punched Gabe in the face, not overly hard, but enough to have the wolf coming awake with a feral growl, and attacking Braxas's wrist. Hard. The bond within him flared with strength as the circle formed, and he could see the wound on Gabe's stomach healing before his eyes. His connection to Gabe solidified, as did the mating bond that tied him so completely to Corrine, and he heard her gasp as she no doubt felt the same effects before he slumped in relief.

Gabe would live.

Braxas turned to see Alak grinning at him after Gabe withdrew his teeth and slumped against Corrine. "Smug bastard." He couldn't help but feel grateful for the assist, however, although he was very much going to enjoy seeing Gabe's wrath at being sucker-punched in the face once he recovered.

"It worked, didn't it?" Alak shrugged as if he didn't know what the fuss was all about.

"Aeron," Braxas began, "you said that this connection between Gabe andme would come with enhancements to our physical abilities, right?"

Aeron nodded with a grin as a low growl began to

build around them. Gabe was coming to.

"What fucker with a death wish just punched me in the face?" Gabe's voice was slightly garbled, which was a sure sign that his wolf was close. Braxas flashed a wide toothy smile at Alak, who looked slightly alarmed.

"That would be Alak," Braxas answered cheerfully, and he turned to look at his brother, pleased to see Gabe had lost that pale ashen look, and his eyes flashing with evil intent. "Good to have you back, brother."

Chapter Twenty-Four

Corrine was physically and emotionally exhausted by the time they pulled into the driveway back home. Gabe had tried to reassure her that he was fully healed, but she couldn't stop touching him as if to make certain for herself. It was terrifying to think how things could have changed in the blink of an eye.

"Stop worrying, love." Gabe urged her ahead of him through the back kitchen door. "I'm fine. We're fine."

"Sit down, sweetheart. I'll make you some tea." Braxas placed a quick kiss on her lips before Gabe sat at the cushioned breakfast nook and pulled her in tight to his chest.

"Thank you," she said, smiling back at her mate. Erica and her men walked in just then and joined them at the table with heavy sighs, as did the two Dark Fae.

"So…" Erica looked around before she dug into her pocket and threw the metal cuffs they'd found on Kat onto the table, "where exactly *the fuck* did those weasels get these bad boys?"

Both Alak and Aeron's expressions turned to angry scowls as Alak picked up the cuffs to examine the markings.

"The rogues had these cuffs?" Aeron's eyes fixed on Corrine for confirmation. He looked quite disturbed when she nodded. "There is Dark Fae magic woven into this metal, but it is … odd. The magic has been twisted somehow, or the magic user has. We have not seen this before. The blade that Gabe was wounded with must have come from the same place as these cuffs. This does not bode well."

"Maybe Kat overheard something from Zayden

or Nyx as to where they got these items?" Leo asked.

Corrine noticed for the first time that Katrina was not with them, even though she was supposed to come back with Erica, Leo, and Ben. "Where did she go?" Corrine's chest tightened. She'd been too preoccupied thinking about Gabe to notice that perhaps Kat may have needed some support after the horrible ordeal that she experienced. "Do you think she needs someone to talk to about what she went through?"

"Kat isn't a big 'sharer' actually," Braxas said, setting her tea down in front of her. He then snuggled in on her other side. "She probably just needed some time alone to regroup."

Braxas texted Katrina. His phoned pinged quickly with a short response confirming what Braxas had just told them.

Corrine noticed that the twins had gone oddly still when Katrina's name had come up. She hoped that the earlier confrontation between the three of them wasn't going to get awkward. After all, with this new discovery of dangerous artifacts circling around rogue shifters, it meant that the Dark Fae still had work to do among them.

"We need to speak with our Goddess about this discovery." Alak stood from the table as did his brother. "Excuse us."

"Of course." Corrine nodded at them as they left through the back door to the patio before she turned to her mates. "I don't know about you guys, but I would do anything right about now for an hour in that Jacuzzi tub upstairs."

"Go relax, baby." Braxas kissed her gently before he stood and gave her untouched tea a considering look. "We've got a few more things to discuss here. How about I upgrade that tea to a glass of wine with your bath?"

She smiled shyly at his attentiveness. It was still a bit surreal that these two wonderful men were hers alone. The mate bond among them flowed freely now, and Braxas was using it to his full advantage in gauging what she needed. Corrine vowed to herself that she would spend the rest of her life doing the same for her two men. She hoped that all this madness would soon come to an end so that they could find some time just for the three of them.

"Wine would be perfect, my love."

****

The wine *had* been perfect, especially combined with the soothing hot water. By the time Gabe and Braxas had come upstairs to join her, Corrine had almost been asleep. Her thoughtful men had plucked her out of the bath, dried her off, and tucked her safely in between them where she fell into a content slumber.

Corrine woke up to an empty bed, the next morning, but she felt fully rested and ready to attack the day—whatever it may hold in store. She quickly dressed and bounced down the stairs, motivated by the undeniable aromas of coffee and bacon coming from the kitchen.

"Morning, love." Gabe's smile when he saw her made her heart flutter in her chest. "You're just in time. Braxas was about to make some of his *famous* waffles."

She laughed at the air quotes and teasing eye roll her wolf gave her, and she gave both her mates a morning kiss before grabbing a coffee and joining Erica, Ben, and Leo at the kitchen table.

"Heathen, you know nothing of waffles." Braxas threw a strawberry at Gabe's head before turning his attention back to his batter.

"Of course I don't. Real men eat pancakes." Gabe

winked at her, causing both her and Erica to laugh.

"Well, I hate to break it to you, Alpha," Leo's nose lifted to scent the air as Braxas poured the first batch of batter onto the waffle iron, "but I've had your pancakes, and they don't smell near as good as what the cat has got cooking."

"Traitor," was all Gabe mumbled back as his own nose rose to investigate the warm vanilla scent. Then he turned back to finish cooking the omelets he was preparing.

The patio door opened and Aeron and Alak entered, looking exhausted and still wearing their same clothes from the day before.

"Have you guys been out there all night?" Erica asked as they took seats at the table. Ben got up to get them some coffee.

"The discussion with our Lady Ryssana was complex." Aeron gave Ben a grateful smile as he took the hot cup of coffee that was offered. "She has declared it more important now than ever that we stay here and discover the source of these dark enchanted weapons."

Corrine had already suspected this outcome.

"She has also requested your presence, Queen Eyrica of the Light Fae, at our village," Alak said. "You and your mates must go there today."

"Oh?" Erica seemed surprised, and then curiosity lit her eyes. "We would love to see the village and meet more of your people." She then added, "And please call me Erica."

"Ishaya will be waiting for you at noon at the gate. He will take you on the journey." Aeron smiled at her. "Erica."

"Uh-oh," Gabe chuckled, "are you making them take the long route?"

"Our Goddess has said that Erica and her mates

are now our people as well, and can be trusted with the true path to our homes. By taking the footpath in the forest they will be able to find their way without an escort should they need to."

"The village is beautiful, Eyrica. You'll love it." Corrine smiled at her former charge. She then slipped away to hit the washroom before breakfast was ready. She was feeling very optimistic that Light and Dark Fae were finally coming together once again.

When she came back out, the boys were just setting the food out along the island countertop.

"Eat up, baby." Gabe gave her a quick pat on the ass, making her jump before he handed her a warm plate. "Erica has asked that we come with them to the village today, so you'll need your energy for the journey."

"I'd really appreciate the company, Quenya." Erica smiled before she began to fill her own plate.

"Of course." Corrine's heart warmed at Erica's affectionate term. She was happy to get a chance to go back to the forest folk village and see her new friends. She'd take Misha and Laiyla some chocolate just like she had promised and introduce them to Erica. But there was also a small part of her that wished she could just have some quiet time alone with her men.

Oh well. There will be many years ahead for that, she supposed.

****

Three hours later, they were walking through the woods caravan style, on their way to the Veil portal. This time, however, they had fully stocked backpacks and were ready for a two-day journey through the woods. The importance of toilet paper could *not* be trivialized.

Corrine may have gotten over exuberant with the number of gifts and treats she'd packed for the village folk, but Ben had been a sweetheart and offered to take it all in his backpack for her.

"Here we are," Erica announced as she stopped in front of the mountainside that housed the portal they usually used to cross over. "Hold onto your knickers, gentlemen."

Erica winked at Corrine and then raised her arms to trace out the Fae symbols that would allow them entrance, and one by one, they disappeared into the mist.

"Ishaya, it's so good to see you!" Corrine pulled the large man in for a hug once they were safely on the other side.

"And you, Lady Corrine." His deep rumble echoed around them. "Now, let's be off, you three." She felt confusion at his words since clearly there were six of them joining him. "We need to get a decent distance before sundown. Can't have this trip taking up too much of my fishing time, now can we?"

"I trust you know the way, friends?" Ishaya asked Gabe and Braxas. Then he shook hands with them both. "Oh, and everything is set as you requested."

She was beginning to get the feeling like she was the only one who didn't know what was going on when Erica gave her a wink and a quick hug. She then followed behind Ishaya and her mates into the forest, leaving the three of them behind.

"Spill. What's going on?" she asked, turning back to her men with her hands on her hips.

"It's a surprise, baby." Gabe laughed at her stance before he pulled a blindfold out of his back pocket and held it up for her. "Are you game?"

Braxas took her backpack from her with a devious smile and a wave of arousal washed over her skin, causing goosebumps to rise along her body.

She smiled, then turned around, allowing Gabe to

slip the covering over her eyes. Each man took one of her hands and led her along until she could hear the soothing sound of falling water. Corrine hoped that she guessed correctly where they were, and when the blindfold was removed, she gasped at what she saw in front of her.

A full picnic had been set up on the grass near the waterfall where they had first made love, and next to that, she saw a little lean-to made out of wood. Inside, was a luxurious looking pallet complete with pillows and a fluffy down duvet. Her eyes filled with tears as she took in the chilling champagne and plates filled with her favorite foods. Gabe and Braxas had somehow known that she wanted time just for the three of them, and they had pulled out all the stops to make it a magical night. They had made her speechless.

"Love," Braxas tilted her head up to look into her eyes, "why are you crying? Don't you like your surprise?"

"I'm just so ... happy." She sniffled as both of their arms came around her. "I've never really been happy before, at least not in a very long time. My visions led me to see such horrible things, and there were so many times that I almost gave up hope that I ever would be."

"I feel truly happy, too, baby." Gabe leaned in to nuzzle at her neck from behind her. "The future we have now justifies everything we went through to get here. It's beyond my wildest dreams, and I don't want to waste a second of it."

"I agree." Braxas drew back and took her hand to lead her towards the makeshift bed. "We have been blessed by the Gods and Goddesses, and Gabe and I will spend the rest of our lives making sure the gift of your love is never taken for granted."

"But for right now, you're wearing far too many clothes to allow us to worship you properly," Gabe added before he stripped off his shirt and nodded for her to do the same.

Corrine quickly undressed so she could concentrate on watching her beautiful mates reveal their hard, golden bronzed skin. Her fingers traced over Gabe's chest, loving how warm his skin felt against her own, and when his pants quietly settled around his ankles, she dropped to her knees in front of him and wrapped her fingers around his erect shaft, making him groan her name.

"Baby, I can't think when you touch me," Gabe panted as she leaned in further and ran her tongue over the swollen head of his cock.

She felt Braxas's huge hands run down her naked back slowly before they came to rest on her ass. He massaged the globes and urged her to lift her hips and spread her legs apart.

"Just keep doing what you're doing, love," Braxas murmured before she felt his warm breath against her now exposed womanhood. "Don't mind me."

His first long lick all along the length of her swollen folds had her moaning as she took Gabe's shaft into her mouth, her grip tightening around the part of him she couldn't swallow.

"I'm not sure that's a possibility, brother," Gabe chuckled and then moaned as she renewed her efforts, taking him into her mouth and using her tongue to caress every inch of him she could. "Sweet Goddess, but just keep on doing it."

Braxas nibbled and ate her pussy like he was a starving man, circling his tongue around her clit to tease before moving away to lick at the juices her body was producing for him. She tried to move her hips to get his mouth where she needed it most, but his hands gripped her and took control.

"Uh-uh, baby," Gabe whispered, his hands coming to rest on her shoulders. "You take what Braxas gives you like a good girl."

She drew hard on his cock in apology, causing him to curse and thrust his hips forward making her gag a little.

"I'm losing control here, Braxas." Gabe thrust between her lips once again. "I think it's time for a change in positions."

Braxas murmured back before he finally wrapped his soft lips around Corrine's swollen clit and suckled, taking her almost to the peak of climax. Her body tensed, waiting to fall over into glorious sensation, her breath sticking in her chest. And then his mouth was suddenly gone, leaving her to fall back down to Earth, unsatisfied.

Before she could voice her disappointment, she felt the hot, wet, head of his cock nudge up against her soaking folds, and slowly he filled her up in one long thrust that took her breath away.

"Oh Goddess, you feel so good around me, love." He slowly moved in and out of her. "Gabe, help lift her up."

Braxas held still, his hands on her hips keeping his hard shaft deep inside of her while Gabe pulled himself free of her mouth and lifted her until she was sitting on Braxas's folded legs, her back up against his warm chest. Immediately, one of his hands left her hip to encase her breast, teasing and plucking at the nipple. Corrine's eyes moved up to meet Gabe's and she smiled at the love and tenderness she saw revealed in them.

He leaned in to softly place a kiss along her collarbone, then continued, making his way gently up her neck and all over her face before he finally reached her lips.

Braxas had been kissing her along the other side of her neck, and the sheer emotion she felt through their mating bond brought tears to her eyes.

Gabe's mouth moved gently on hers as Braxas's hips slowly began to move again, stroking in and out of her at a slow pace. They continued that way for what felt like an eternity until the man behind her finally drew all the way out of her soaking passage. Without a word, Gabe released her mouth and moved his hands down to place his rigid length, which had been rubbing along her stomach, into position before he slid home with a sigh. Braxas turned Corrine's head so that he now was able to plunder her mouth the same way that Gabe had just done.

She moaned at the feel of his wet cock, now rubbing between the cheeks of her ass, and she ached for him to press in and fill her up while Gabe moved inside of her as well.

"Please, Braxas," she moaned in between his slow and devastating kisses, his hands moving all over her, creating a haze of fire in her blood that could only be quenched by having both of her mates inside of her. "I need you both ... please."

He teased her by rubbing his hard cock head over her rosette, stopping to put just enough pressure to tease her before he moved on, sliding himself along her warm flesh.

"I think we've teased our mate enough, don't you, brother?" Gabe's voice sounded strained as he continued his torturous pace inside of her.

"Yes, please." She groaned and tightened her muscles around him, causing his hips to buck.

Corrine felt Braxas line himself up with her hole before he gently grasped her chin to look deep into her eyes.

"I have never felt more alive and content than I do when I am a part of you, my love." He slowly pushed inside, and she exhaled as she let him in and felt the bliss of being connected to both of the men she loved.

Only a moment passed before they began to move inside of her, alternating their strokes, bringing her body to a fever pitch of sensations. The more vocal she got, the harder they loved her. There wasn't another noise in the entire world save for the sound of their skin slapping against hers and the moans of their desire. Corrine felt the heat growing low in her center, muscles contracting, getting ready to explode in the glorious nirvana of release. It was almost *too* much pleasure. Her brain couldn't keep up with the sensations as Gabe's cock thrust deep into her pussy, only leaving to then make room for Braxas's thick shaft to take its place easing into her ass.

Then finally the moment came—her breath caught in her chest as her entire body detonated in a fury of unleashed pleasure. It permeated every single cell of her being, making her feel as though she had been lifted from her reality and flung into the heavens as she screamed her pleasure for the world to hear.

She could feel her mates follow her over in their own orgasms, their muscles tightening, bodies wrapped around hers. Corrine must have grabbed each of their hands because she felt her fingers twined around theirs, the three of them connected in a way that was truly divine.

When she opened her eyes, it was to both of her mates, the warm golden eyes of her cougar and the sky-blue eyes of her wolf.

"From now until eternity, love." Braxas kissed

her before letting Gabe do the same.

As Corrine lay in the arms of the two men she never dreamed could be hers, she knew that the Goddesses truly did have a plan for them all. She had learned that despite the pain of her journey, if she held fast to what she believed in and stood up for what was right, then the rewards would be far greater than she could ever have imagined.

Epilogue

Braxas couldn't stop smiling after the night he and Gabe had shared with Corrine. They had made love to her several more times throughout the night, and as promised, one of those times had been under the soothing waterfall. He cursed the morning, wishing they didn't have to leave, but Grahame would be waiting for them at his house to take them directly to the village to meet up with the others.

He knew they did not have much time to linger in the Fae Realm, as important pack matters required their almost immediate attention. Before they left, the rogues who had been transported to pack property, had shifted their allegiance and were given temporary sanctuary. Some rogues had managed to escape amidst the chaos, but whether they'd rejoined his cousin Zayden and his cowardly sidekick Nyx, still remained to be seen.

Braxas knew his cousin well enough to expect him to regroup. The fact that they were able to gain access to Dark objects also had him concerned. Something much bigger was headed their way soon. Braxas could feel it. He only hoped that they would be ready to face it together.

He wasn't at all surprised that the rogues who'd defected to their side knew very little about the objects obtained. A few of them had heard rumors though about an underground market that was held in constantly changing locations, and they were puzzled as to why shifters would seek out weapons in the first place.

What *was* surprising was finally getting to see some of the effects their new triad mating had produced. It seemed that Braxas's pard had responded to Gabe's Alpha authority as they responded to him. It was the same with how Gabe's pack members responded to Braxas now. Before the exchange of blood between himself and Gabe, the pack and pard simply acknowledged the other's authority as a form of respect and allegiance. They were truly unified now. He supposed it would work much the same with having two Betas and so forth in the chain of authority, but his theory would have to be tested later when his brooding Kat returned.

His fierce Beta had been hurt pretty badly, and yet, he knew she was out there, already on his cousin's trail. He suspected that her immediate disappearance into her work might have also had to do with her reaction to the two High Dorum and theirs to her. He made a mental note to get to the bottom of that with her when she returned. He'd reassure her that they could be trusted. They both may be arrogant know-it-alls, he thought—especially Alak, but he knew they were also good men.

He, Gabe, and Corrine ate breakfast quickly and then packed up their things after reluctantly getting dressed. Grahame was already waiting for them before the turnoff to his house. He failed miserably at hiding his knowing smirk.

"I trust you had a pleasant evening?" he asked.

"I imagine ours was a bit more interesting than fishing," Corrine saucily replied, making all three men chuckle. "Will you be meeting up with Ishaya there?"

"Indeed," Grahame said.

Healthy this time around and without taking too much time to rest along the way, they were able to make the journey in a day and a half. As they entered the village, it seemed to be abuzz with activity. Villagers headed in every direction, stopping to talk to their neighbors. There hadn't been so much activity the last time they had been here.

"There have been whisperings from the Goddess, more so of late," Grahame remarked on the scene. "There must be some sort of development."

It certainly *was* quite the development, Braxas observed when they finally arrived at the only two-story structure in the village, that upon closer inspection, turned out to be a meeting place for the Dorum council.

It looked very much like someone's house from the outside, the face of the building comprised of inviting yellow brick, trimmed grass and bushes, colorful flowers that Braxas had never seen anywhere else other than this side of the Veil, and a paved walkway leading up to an ornately carved wooden door. Inside, however, the small foyer led into a grand room with high ceilings and a candlelit chandelier. Instead of pews, there were rows of either cushy looking chairs or couches facing the front. There was no podium in the front of the large room, only more comfortable looking couches.

Though the place actually looked like it would be a very relaxed meeting place, the atmosphere in the room was currently anything but at the moment. Loud arguing voices rang around the room, some for, some against, and some undecided, though it took a few moments for Braxas to see what all the fuss was about.

He heard Corrine gasp just before she ran up to the first-row seating area where Erica and her men currently occupied one of the couches. He and Gabe began to make their way up to the front of the room, and as they got closer, it all became suddenly clear.

Erica sat with a baby in her arms. Leo huddled close on one side of her, and Ben, who sat on the other side of her, was also holding a baby. By the pale gray tone of the children's skin, he guessed that these must be the orphaned twins they'd been told about.

He saw Erica looking down at the bundle in her arms, then glancing at the other bundle with a besotted, dreamy look upon her face. She seemed not to be paying attention to any of the proceedings as her men, as well as Alak and Aeron, argued passionately, in favor of the trio adopting the babies.

"Our Goddess has willed it so," Aeron declared to the crowd.

"Do you dare to go against her will?" Alak asked the opposition.

Braxas noticed how even though the opposition still looked obstinate, they were not unaffected when the two High Dorum spoke. Braxas equated this to how shifters responded to their Alphas.

"We cannot allow these Dark Fae children to be raised by *their kind*," said one angry woman, pointing a finger at Erica, Ben, and Leo, her tattoos moving across her arms as she argued. "Our Goddess is the one who separated us from their kind. Did she not?"

"And with good reason," added a man sitting next to her. "They are selfish beings. Our children should be raised by their own kind."

"Selfish?" Alak roared. "That woman," he pointed at Erica, "nearly sacrificed her life, and *did* sacrifice her ability to bear children in order to protect her people from a tyrant. Those men beside her are shifters, not Fae, and yet they nearly died as well for the Fae cause."

"The time for separatism to come to an end is upon us," Aeron added. "It is time for us all to band together if we are to survive what has been foreseen."

"I am inclined to agree with you, cousins," came a soft-spoken voice from the back of the room.

"Thank you, Aneena," Aeron said.

But it appeared that their cousin had more to say.

"Though I agree with you about bringing our peoples together, including shifter kind, and I have no doubt as to the bravery and selflessness of Lady Erica and her mates, nor do I question their ability to be good parents, they have no experience with our kind."

Braxas saw no judgment in her eyes, only a deep sadness for these children. Braxas remembered hearing that she was the one who had saved them and blamed herself for not being able to save their parents as well.

"Our Goddess told you to bring the Queen and her Kings of the Light Fae here to the village so that we may begin to bring our people together. She told you to show them the babies, to place them in their arms, and then what? How can we be sure that this trio is the right choice to raise these children? How will they know how to deal with their gifts when they emerge?"

It was Erica who answered, her voice barely above a whisper, but nonetheless sure in her response. "Because I already feel them in my very soul. They are our fate." And then, as any loving mother would, she leaned down and softly kissed the head of the baby she was holding, before doing the same to one that Ben held.

The End

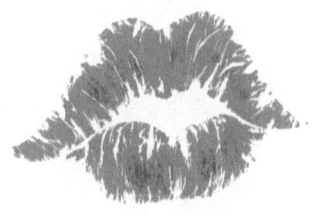

EVERNIGHT PUBLISHING ®

www.evernightpublishing.com